White house

Victor Lugala

ISBN: 978-0-9876141-0-0

Published by: Africa world books, Perth, Australia
Edited by Cheryl Bettridge AE and Catherine Schwerin

Design and typesetting of text: All In One Book Design
Cover design: Rob Rooker

Acknowledgements

This story of love and agony is a true survivor. A thief stole the few pages of the initial draft. Professor Taban lo Liyong, who taught me many things, told me not to cry over spilt milk, but to scrape the bottom of the pot to move the story forward. Then Professor Mairi John Blackings read the finished draft. If the thief must be put to shame, it is, thanks to Atem Yaak Atem, whose emails from Australia always nudged me to write longer stories like this, for he too, tasted the pudding at the preparatory stage.

It is 1992, the year that God wept for Juba. A dark curtain descended on the town and red terror threatened to suffocate the civilian population. There was widespread starvation, fear, hatred, suspicion, and quick death. Human life was of little value, if not valueless. In the main ghost house men stripped half naked and emaciated beyond recognition were chained to their fate, waiting forlornly, dejectedly, for the dark hour, when the executioner's hammer would crush and shatter their skulls. Their graves no living creature could identify with certainty without running mad from the sight of a rugged hill of bones, old and new.

◆

It is wartime and Juba airport is a sardine can of humanity. These are civilians at the precipice of life, for they will soon become refugees in their own country. Here they are, waiting to board a cargo plane to Khartoum, the country's capital city, and from there, if they are lucky enough, they will proceed beyond the country's borders, to other peaceful lands where they could hopefully live happily while nursing sweet memories of home, a home that was now occupied by soldiers of fortune.

Women cuddling breastfeeding babies, young people in their prime and sick-looking people burdened with earthly troubles locked in their heads were all waiting to travel by air, most of them for the first time. They were running away from a town they hated to leave but had no choice to live in, either.

The cargo plane was the only means of transport linking Juba in the south and Khartoum in the north. From the north the plane transported soldiers of fortune, mercenaries, guns, ammunition, bad luck and explosives to feed the hungry war theatre in the south. The cargo plane went back to the north with a human cargo, so to speak, including wounded soldiers and sometimes raw teak looted from the forest reserves. The passengers sat on the floor of the plane like bags. They boarded the cargo plane free because they could not afford an air ticket, let alone food, which had become scarce. In a way the military regime wanted to hold these people hostage of the system by encouraging them to seek refuge in the north rather than them running or escaping to the bush behind rebel lines.

On the runway of the airport a Boeing 707 cargo plane squatted like a toad. Some military cargo was hurriedly offloaded into military trucks that drove away very fast. The airport lounge was humid and musty. The passengers sweated profusely. The women fanned their little ones with crumpled pieces of cloth or headscarves. Some of the old men scraped the sweat from their foreheads with bent forefingers. The passengers' eyes and minds were transfixed on the huge toad that would carry them many miles away, to Khartoum, into internal refuge, or beyond.

Amidst the din a casually dressed skinny northern Sudanese with a mop of dark hair and a heavy moustache briskly walked into the lounge. He carried some papers and a red megaphone. With the blazing eyes of a snake he quickly scanned the black faces in the lounge. Without wasting time he blew air into the megaphone. The megaphone crackled.

"Attention, attention, everybody!" shouted the man in a croaky voice as if he had a hangover. His Arabic sounded typically Khartoumish.

"If you are travelling to Khartoum and you are sure your name is on the list, listen! And listen carefully. When I call your name and you know it is your name, move quickly and form a straight line near the main exit, ready to board. If your name is not on my list you have no business loitering around."

When the man called the names of the passengers there was subdued silence, except for children coughing or sneezing or crying for a mother's teat. The desperate-looking people wanted to be sure that their names were on the list. As soon as the man finished calling out the names of the passengers, a long, crooked queue of passengers bearing pitiable hand luggage had already formed. They were ready and anxious to board the cargo plane. Some of the people were sweating nervously. There was, however, a group of young men standing, murmuring and wondering why their names were not on the list. The man with the heavy moustache noticed them. He looked at them hard, threateningly, then pointed at them, his index finger almost shaking. They were five in all. They did not know who the man was pointing at, so they looked at each other askance.

"Blue shirt," shouted the man, "Step out!"

The young man wearing the blue shirt carried a rucksack on his back like a fat baby. He timidly walked with unsteady steps to meet the man who looked like Mr Bad News.

"What's your name?" the man asked.

"Riti," said the young man in the blue shirt.

The man quickly raced his bloodshot eyes through the list and announced: "Riti. Riti. Riti does not exist in this world."

He gave Riti a serious look as if expecting a reply.

"Were you here yesterday?" he asked.

Riti nodded.

"Were you here the day before?"

Riti nodded again.

"Were you here last week?"

Riti nodded again, this time his chin rose and fell on his chest, shaking.

"Look Mr blue shirt," said the man, "I don't want to see your face again anywhere near the airport, understand? Get lost!"

The legacy of war was the nightmare suffered by southern Sudanese men in Juba. If they survived death they lived on borrowed time. They suffered mental torture, and if they didn't go mad their manhood was crushed. Love and sex, however, were the delicate and precious readily available commodities that lived side by side with war. Palliatives, if you like. Love and sex were the medicine of the heart shared by enemies and their victims alike. And jealousy was rife. The civilian men who decided to remain in Juba during the war buried their heads in the warm bosoms of women and girlfriends. Some of the vile women who knew the vulnerability of men used sex as a weapon of war.

◆

The building housing *Juba Times* weekly newspaper was situated along Government Road, about two kilometres from downtown Juba. The office was nestled among neem trees, surrounded with a creeping hedge. There were a few cacti, jacaranda and acacia trees scattered in the compound. The flowerbed that had some white lilies, violets and bougainvillea cried for the caring hands of the gardener who never returned to work a couple of months ago. The photography section of the newspaper was on the first floor of the one-storey colonial building. Riti's desk was close to a large, Gothic window overlooking Juba airport. The window gave a panoramic view of the expansive landscape beyond the airport. In the wet season the landscape was lush, except for the airport runway which was a paste of black tar.

During the dry season a large flock of heron perched in the mango trees by the river Nile, near Gabat slum, home to the lepers who begged for alms in the streets by day and pushed opium in their shacks by night. During the hot season the Gothic window inhaled some breeze to cool the photography section.

The window opened into the world of Riti's wild and distant imagination and fantasy. At one time he saw himself as a successful photographer exhibiting his works in museums of modern art in London, Paris and Rome. At other times he was fishing on the banks of the river Yangtze among grinning rural Chinese with tobacco-stained teeth. At yet other times he saw his haggard self in the mirror of his heart, which was trapped in an unyielding war zone, wheezing under the heavy weight of oppression. Sometimes he saw himself as a recruit in the ranks and file of the rebel forces who were fighting the military regime in power to free southerners from subjugation. The window was a source of melancholy and some nostalgia, especially when he reminisced about the old Juba, when the only sounds familiar to his ears were the Cathedral bells, braying donkeys, cockcrows, bicycle bells, street hawkers and the laughter of girls carrying water in plastic jerrycans on their heads. As if it had grown old within the shortest time and space, nowadays all he heard in his mind was the angry clap of automatic rifles, grinding army boots and, in the dark sometimes the midnight silence was interrupted by the blowing wind, which whispered the macabre sound of imminent death.

◆

On Monday morning Riti went to work very early. His harassment at the airport the previous day was like a wake-up call. He did not sleep. He was awake the whole night, tossing on his ribs, thinking about the direction of his life. He struggled to reassure himself that his river of life would continue to flow with few rapids as long as he breathed the oxygen of hope. By all accounts he was shaken by Sunday's encounter at the airport.

The office smelled of bat droppings. The ceiling of the office was a safe haven for a flock of bats as if they eavesdropped on people's conversations in the newsroom. The floor was dusty. The high ceiling fan was frozen since the generators of the Juba Electricity Corporation ran out of fuel a couple of years ago.

When Riti remembered the aversion he received from the plain-clothes skinny man at the airport the previous day, he felt like an alien in his own hometown, and the more he felt isolated psychologically the more he wished he could join the rebels. The clandestine rebel radio was a great influence on him and other young people of his age. He was twenty three years old. He listened to their daily broadcasts religiously but in hiding, fearful of the security that had eyes and ears stuck in every corner of Juba, including his workplace. It was whispered that some informers had infiltrated the newsroom. As if to substantiate the rumour at least two of his colleagues had been picked up by security and disappeared under mysterious circumstances. Everybody in the office seemed to cast glances over their shoulders as if to ask, 'Who is next?' Such unuttered questions removed Riti from the society to which he was supposed to belong, associate and relate. Some of his friends and acquaintances had fled the town. Some had either gone to the bush to fight in the liberation war or fled to relative safety in the north of the vast country. Going into exile seemed a lot easier and more appealing than going behind rebel lines, which was very, very risky. That was why his mind raced into exile while his physical body suffered political oppression in Juba.

In the days to come, Riti would continue to look through the Gothic window of the office, and each time he saw the cargo plane land or leave the airport, he would long for the day and hour he would depart Juba and go to Khartoum, into exile, or if he chose, he would use a long detour to go to the bush to fight in the liberation struggle.

◆

It was a sizzling Friday afternoon. The air in the newsroom was suffocating. Owing to the fact that the ceiling fan had stopped functioning two years ago some of the reporters fanned themselves with old newspapers. Riti had just submitted his photo essay to the editor and was on his feet ready to trek home to the suburbs where ordinary folks lived from hand to mouth. He lived with his widowed mother and only sister in a compound with two houses. The houses were fairly old with rusty, corrugated iron roofing and adobe bricks for walls. His mother and sister lived in one of these and he lived in a smaller one. A low-roofed shack served as a kitchen and store.

In the 1990s Atlabara suburb was at the heart of Juba and that heart also bled profusely from fresh war wounds. The suburb was divided into three zones: Atlabara A, Atlabara B and Atlabara C. People who lived in Atlabara A were regarded as middle class by the standards of Juba of the time. They were well to do, so to speak. Their houses were semi-permanent with corrugated iron roofs and brick walls, although they looked old after years of not having been painted or renovated. Some of the houses in Atlabara A had piped water, electricity and outdoor pit latrines. In wartime some semblance of affluence could only be discerned from the environment that sported carcasses of vehicles sitting on rocks. Some of the concrete perimeter walls or bamboo fences were on the verge of collapse and some had collapsed after a rainstorm.

The inhabitants of Atlabara B and C, on the other hand, shared the same misery of living from hand to mouth or struggling to survive. Their houses lacked the amenities enjoyed by their neighbours in

Atlabara A. They toiled at the edge of society. The women cooked their food with firewood and the community eased itself in the nearby stream. Most dwellings in Atlabara B and C were tukuls, conical grass-thatched roofs, with mud walls that smelled of cow dung and abject poverty, with cockroaches, ticks, and rats as their immediate neighbours. Given a choice these inhabitants would have migrated to live in the houses of their dreams or of their neighbours in Atlabara A but they were slaves of their social fate.

Atlabara acquired its name for the wrong reasons from another era of war, during the Anyanya war of liberation in the 1960s. Following the burning of Juba in 1965 by Arab soldiers it was alleged that there was a door-to-door search for what they called mutineers or Anyanya elements. Men were dragged out of their houses and shot dead in front of their loved ones. Whenever the soldiers entered a compound they would ask, "Are there men inside the house?" If the family members responded in the affirmative, the soldiers would shout, "*Atla bara*", meaning "get out" in Arabic. Despite the negative memories of a bygone war, the abominable name of the suburb stuck like superglue, and the echoes of that era were to resonate three decades later when the current war erupted and some men were still being removed from their homes and dragged into the night on a journey of no return.

Riti lived in Atlabara A. His late father was a civil servant who had acquired the piece of land that was to become life's surety for the small family now without a family head.

Riti arrived home soaked in sweat. His white cotton shirt was plastered to his wiry body. He removed the shirt and hung it on a nail on the wall. He rested his frame on the bed and switched on the radio. He turned down the volume of the radio and pinned it to his ear so he could listen to the latest news on the clandestine rebel radio station. Sometimes the regime jammed the broadcasts on the rebels' radio to deprive listeners in Juba who could be influenced by the rebel propaganda machine. Sometimes people found openly listening to the clandestine radio broadcasts were arrested and beaten up by security.

As Riti listened to the radio with one ear, the other ear heard something sinister in the compound. He switched off the radio and placed it under the bed. He heard somebody sobbing in the kitchen. When he peeped through his door he saw a young lady being comforted by his mother and sister. The young lady was married for only a few months to a neighbour who was a police officer. Riti knew her and her husband. They played dominoes together at the Atlabara Youth Club. Out of curiosity he put on a t-shirt and walked to the kitchen. When he saw Leila, for that was the name of the neighbour's wife, her cheeks were rivers of tears and more tears were flowing. Her eyes were now red.

"Leila," Riti whispered. "What happened?" But Riti's question invited more tears. Riti looked disturbed.

"Did your husband beat you?" He ventured. The husbands of Juba were known for venting their social frustration on their wives. In a quiet response Leila shook her head. She was shaking. Nervous. Her dress was dusty, as if she had rolled on the ground like a traditional mourner.

Looking at his mother Riti whispered, "Does Leila bring bad news that I have not heard?"

Riti's mother whispered in response, "It is Ben, her husband."

"What happened?" he asked. Leila gained some courage and whispered, "They took him away. They took away my only Ben."

"Where did they take him?" Riti asked. Leila pushed out her tongue and with it she pointed in the direction where the sun sets, that could only mean the white house, a misnomer for Juba's dreaded ghost house. Men in plain clothes manhandled Ben in the street near the market, bundled him into a Black Maria and drove away with him on the road that led to the army barracks, south of Atlabara, where the dreaded so-called white house was also located. Seeing the signs of red terror getting closer to home, Riti quietly returned to his room. He thought about Ben, dominoes and the youth club, and got scared. Will he come back at all like one lucky soul among many who were taken to that house? What will the mood be like around the domino table at the club? Will he, Riti, go back to play dominoes at the club? Riti thought and thought, bewildered.

◆

The government was the main employer as most private companies had pulled out, because it had become impossible for them to continue to invest in the war zone. The central government in Khartoum was using or misusing a huge sum of the national budget to perpetuate the war, either in the form of military hardware, paying mercenaries or espionage. It, however, made it difficult to explain if the expense in the war theatre was largely responsible for the chronic delay in salaries of civil servants, especially in the southern regions. Civil servants went without salaries for up to three months. Civil servants had to survive by buying essential commodities such as sugar, salt, oil, grain etc on credit, so much so that when they were paid their salary arrears, it all went to paying the accumulated debts. Given the fact that some of the civil servants had either joined the ranks and file of the rebels and some had died, it was expected that civil servants would receive their salaries on time. But who said the names of the dead civil servants and those who joined the rebellion were struck off the payroll? The ghost names lined the pockets of accountants and bookkeepers who were the moneyed lords of Juba. They were powerful. Although the soldiers and informers were regularly paid their salaries, they were more powerful than the accountants; they carried the gun and terror. They were a law unto themselves. The accountants, bookkeepers, soldiers and tax collectors showed off their ill-gotten money in the beer halls where the war-weary souls drowned their sorrow. An ordinary man who made the mistake of sharing a woman with one of these very powerful men would not live to regret it. They were picked and labelled rebels, fifth columnists, Anyanya rebels.

Rujal-mafi was the main open-air market in the Atlabara area of Juba. It was an African market with a few corrugated iron roofing and brick shops and the rest of the shades were makeshift, either built with timber, cardboard or bamboo, with tin roofs that had rusted with age. The crammed beer halls that stood shoulder to shoulder had mud walls and rusted corrugated iron roofs. The bars had urinals that were nothing but open-roofed, round structures wrapped with gunny sacks or bamboo. The urinals served both men and women. When the men stood inside the urinals their shoulders and heads showed, but it was difficult to know if a woman was inside the structure as one could only tell by the distinct sound of the sharp-shooting urine drilling the bare ground. On pay days the urinals were covered with shovelfuls of ash to soak the overflowing urine. Despite the misery in the suburbs the beer halls teemed with life. By midday the multiple loudspeakers blared with African music. Congolese music was the staple that pulled scores of drinkers to the beer halls. Lonely women who sought the company of men and lonely men who sought the company of women met in the beer halls to make themselves feel at home away from home. The new but dreaded wasting illness had arrived in Juba and was slowly stealing lives. In the beer halls the moneyed patrons dismissed the thief of lives as the disease of *kawajat* or white people, but when the disease started attacking and claiming the lives of the money lords, ordinary people whispered, "The bad one has started knocking on the doors of the rich thieves. The most powerful thief of all is stealing the lives of money thieves. Can't their bags of money buy for them a cure even in faraway India?"

Riti's elder sister, Bianca, owned a bar in Rujal-mafi market. They called her *sheikha*, a title bestowed upon a female bar owner. Although the moniker was often bestowed upon elderly women the

age of Bianca's mother, she earned it by virtue of being an entre-
preneur. Whispers from the lips of jealous women indicated that
she didn't honestly acquire the capital for starting her business.
Even her brother, Riti, had his reserved doubts that he couldn't
articulate, as after all she was contributing generously towards the
family upkeep. Sometimes when his salary was delayed she gave
him pocket money. She once bought Riti's girlfriend a handbag as
a birthday present. In wartime Juba it was a select group of young
women who had become powerful. They had access to cash, which
in most cases was obtained through dubious means. It was anybody's
guess that the moneyed lords, informers and soldiers showered the
young ladies with cash for two reasons, to get love in return or to
inform them about suspected rebels in their neighbourhoods. The
informers or secret agents who were of fair complexion and wavy
hair were conspicuous in the suburbs and therefore found it difficult
to penetrate the local communities without their mere presence
raising suspicion. Therefore, women who sold tea by the roadside or
marketplaces and sellers of alcohol were said to be doubling up as
freelance informers. It was often rumoured that these women were
worse than the real informers. Some of the women were driven by
malice, hatred, revenge or sheer jealousy.

If Riti's sister Bianca was indeed a beneficiary of the moneyed lords
it followed that she was either in love with one of these men or she was
indeed a freelance informer, which made no difference because the
concubine of an informer could be obliged to volunteer some information, especially if she was benefiting materially.

Bianca must be sleeping with the enemy. And if she is sleeping
with the enemy she herself must be an enemy within. And who
knows, maybe she is already carrying a seed in her womb, a poisonous
seed that will destroy us all? Riti's comprehensive thoughts about his
sister made him bitter. He recalls that one late evening, notwithstanding the night curfew, Bianca was dropped at home in a car

which even in the dark could only have been a military vehicle, as these were the only vehicles that drove throughout Juba at night on night patrol. Because it was dark Riti couldn't see the driver who gave his sister the lift but he could tell from the guttural voice that the man was not a native southern Sudanese. The man spoke with a deep Arabic accent which made Juba Arabic sound out of place. Riti was seated outside in the compound when his sister passed by, smelling of heavy, enticing perfume. He was very angry. He plucked up some courage as he wanted to behave like the prefect of his father's household.

"Sister, you are late today. Aren't you afraid of breaking the curfew? And who was that man in the army car?" he demanded.

"Have you become a policeman, a guard or my husband?" Bianca reacted.

Riti removed his slipper and slapped it hard on the ground and said, "I'm the man in this house and I have all the right to ask even if you are my older sister."

Bianca stood in defiance and with hands akimbo she said, "Riti, you want to speak like who in this house? If you are man enough why don't you start by buying a kilo of sugar or meat for your mother?"

◆

The sun was tilting westwards. The sky was clear. A flock of heron was migrating southwards. The shadow of mama Riti's house projected eastwards, providing a cool shade for the two women. Bianca sat on a wooden chair, her legs astride it. She wore a loose dress that made it easy for Sara, Riti's girlfriend, to sit in front of her. Sara sat on a mat and her shoulders were between Bianca's thighs. With one hand Bianca pressed down Sara's bunch of hair, and with the other she held a black and white porcupine bristle with which she made two parallel lines as she neatly plaited Sara's hair.

The two women conversed in low tones and laughed loudly and sarcastically. The topic of conversation was of common interest to them. In Juba such kind of talk between mutual friends, especially women, is referred to as 'focus', more or less a euphemism for gossip.

"How is your 'husband'?" Bianca brought up the matter jokingly. Although Sara and Riti were still dating, Bianca often referred to their relationship as that of husband and wife. Because she got along very well with Sara, she wanted her brother to marry her. She liked her.

"Bianca, my good sister, I should be the one to ask you that question. Seriously, how is he?" Sara asked.

Bianca laughed sarcastically and broke the news.

"I thought he told you that he wanted to travel to Khartoum?"

"Khartoum? Is it the same Khartoum, the capital of the Sudan, or another Khartoum you are talking about? You are kidding me, Bianca. What is Riti going to do in Khartoum without telling me?" Sara was disappointed but appreciated Bianca confiding in her.

"So he wanted to escape to Khartoum and leave me in Juba to rot alone in this heat?"

"He has been going to the airport to get a free lift in one of the cargo planes."

"Then what stopped him from flying? The cargo plane wasn't there or it had developed a mechanical problem? I, the daughter of Kitale, will remain in this Juba of ours. I will remain and remain, and I will get myself a soldier husband who will protect me." Sara was addressing nobody and Bianca felt sorry that she broke the news.

When the two women heard the shuffling of feet in the compound in front of the house, they stopped talking and laughing. It was Leila. She stood for a short while. She preferred to stand as she admired Bianca's handiwork and the hairstyle Sara was getting. She looked weak. Her tender cheeks looked pale as if she had not smeared any lotion on them. She was adjusting to the reality that her husband Ben would not return alive. The family was resigned to his fate. For wasn't it said in Juba that whoever was taken to the white house wouldn't see the sun again? She spat a lot, this Leila, and the other two women acknowledged her condition with knowing smiles, although they pitied her now that she was being referred to as a young widow. It seemed she was expecting.

As soon as Leila went away the two women heard loud, masculine footsteps. Bianca knew the familiar footsteps, even before she saw the long shadow of her brother, Riti. He walked straight behind the house where the two women sat.

"*Assalam aleikum*," he saluted.

"*Aleik assalam*," the two women replied in one voice, but they didn't look at him. He read the mood and tried to create a light moment.

"Whoever sees you, sees a rose flower," he said, addressing himself to Sara. Sara acknowledged his flattery with indifference. After what she just heard from Bianca she was not in the mood for his excessive flattery to save face.

Riti understood why Bianca was cross with him after their exchange the other day but he didn't know why Sara was being sucked into it. He felt the conspiracy on the part of both women. He was crestfallen. All the same he walked to his room, subdued, and even his footsteps faltered.

Presently a dog came from nowhere and lay comfortably on the mat. Sara grabbed a slipper and slapped it on the ribs. "Go away! Who invited you here? Idiot!" She addressed the dog as if she was addressing a human being. The dog was a mere scapegoat, the angry words were not meant for it as the real target had exited the stage.

Now the two women were chuckling.

"Where is my mother-in-law today?" Sara asked Bianca, meaning Bianca's mother.

"Her younger brother, our uncle, is unwell. She went to see him and to take for him some green herbs."

Sara couldn't wait for Bianca to finish plaiting her hair.

"Brand new bride," Bianca joked.

Sara ran to pee before she stormed into Riti's room without knocking on the door. Riti was lying in bed, reading an old magazine. Or he pretended to be reading something. He sensed trouble but played it cool. Sara didn't say anything. She didn't wait to be told where to sit, instead she pulled a stool closer to the bed where Riti was lying. She sat like a man, with legs apart. Her left hand was pressed on her waist and with the other hand she gestured and spoke with authority.

"Welcome back, Mr Riti," she started, her voice full of cynicism.

"You mean from work?" Riti said.

"Oh, ah, so these days you work in Khartoum and return to sleep in Juba? What luxury!" Sara was being sarcastic as she gesticulated, wagging a finger at Riti like a Malakia woman. Riti was calm. He felt betrayed by his own sister, same father, same mother.

"Sweetie, please calm down. What is the matter?" Riti managed to say calmly.

"What? Who are you calling sweetie? Why didn't you go to Khartoum and call the Jallaba women sweetie-sweetie so that your tongue is chopped off by sharia?" Sara was visibly furious.

Riti felt like bursting into laughter but controlled himself from further embarrassment. He considered Sara's behaviour pure aggression on his person and privacy, although between them there was no longer any privacy. He raised himself and sat on the edge of the bed, his knees deliberately touching Sara's. She backed off, drawing back the stool.

"Hey, hey, please keep a safe distance from the daughter of Kitale!" Although she controlled the stage, she was quite afraid of Riti. What if he slaps me? What if he gets up and strangles me? she thought. She kept quiet, but there was corrosive anger in her chest. Her firm breasts rose and fell in tandem with her breathing. Then she burst into tears. Riti was sorry but he liked it this way. He wanted her tears to drown her anger. He had never seen her that angry. This lady really loves me, he thought. He left her to cry until she exhausted her tears. As she shielded her wet face with her left hand she was oblivious to Riti's hand on her lap. Maybe she wanted his assurance that he will not abandon her and run to Khartoum. After buying some time Riti took a towel from a nail on the wall and offered to clean Sara's wet face. She pushed his hand away and he nearly staggered off balance.

"I'm sorry, sweetie, it was the devil again," he pleaded.

It was getting dark outside.

Sara stormed out of Riti's room and the darkness swallowed her like a stray firefly.

◆

That year the land was soaked in blood. The rains failed and the sudden dry spell during the months of July and August appeared as though there was an early onset of the dry season.

That morning the skyline over Juba was hazy, smoky, dusty. The rising sun was a pale orange ball. The skyline had all the visible symptoms of sickness, uncertainty.

It was supposed to be the wet season, but the grass was dry. The trees were reduced to their shameful nakedness, the leaves having fallen off the branches. Dry spells in Juba could be extra dry. People's lips cracked owing to the dryness in the weather and dehydration. The mornings were slightly cold with a raspy wind so it was predictable for the people of Juba that they didn't expect any downpour despite the abrupt change in the weather.

What seemed like a smokescreen curtained the sun from view. The wind began to blow with a whistle. In some people's imagination they heard some faint sound like that of a rusty water pump which went *kpuk kpuk kpuk*. Some people imagined a popping sound. This was followed by what at first sounded like the heavy rumbling of thunder, which almost cleared doubts in people's minds that it was about to rain, although rain clouds were absent. The ground shook. Things were not normal. Some of the senior citizens who knew a thing or two about the volcanic Rejaf Hill south of Juba thought it was an earthquake. The shaking of the ground resonated in their hearts and distant memories.

Chickens cackled in fright and scampered for shelter. Dogs barked continuously, their stiff tails tucked between their hind legs as they ran away to hide. The ground shook again after what became apparent as a series of heightened explosions somewhere in the very heart of Juba.

Juba was exploding. Juba was imploding.

Women grabbed their babies and ran into their *tukuls*. The children were shepherded and forced to lie under beds. People caught up in the streets could be seen running up and down, confused. Others threw themselves in the gutters or on the roadside in case the loud explosions had to do with flying objects like missiles.

This was the first time Juba was rocked with such a series of explosions since the war started eight years ago.

Riti's photo-journalistic instincts told him that Juba was under attack from the east. Through their clandestine radio the rebels of late were repeatedly warning people in Juba of an imminent attack. Could this have been the warning shot? Riti thought. He ran into the street. Did he know where he was running to, or for what? It was just the photo-journalistic instinct that foolishly told him to run against the people running away until he saw one man running away with a wound on his head. His face was wounded and his torn shirt was soaked in blood. His face was full of blood. It was as if a bowl of beef stew was thrown in his face. Although he ran very fast, it was as if he had visibility problems. He ran in a zigzag, missing steps, almost stumbling.

"What is the matter?" Riti stopped to ask the man in distress, but it was as if the man was being told to run faster.

Realising that he didn't have a camera on him, and on seeing the flow of blood, Riti turned back and joined the runners. When he turned the corner to their fence he saw a man on a black motorbike. The engine of the motorbike was off. The man wore dark glasses and smoked a cigarette in a relaxed manner, seemingly unconcerned with what was going on in his surroundings. Riti passed the man without greeting him.

When Riti entered his room his heart sank. He suspected the man on the stationary motorbike to be a security man, an intelligence man, an informer. During the war black Honda motorbikes were exclusively used by state security agents, people who were associated with the dreaded white house. They roamed the town to monitor suspicious movements.

Before he could sit on his bed, he heard another loud bang and the ground shook. He imagined his bed was floating in the room. Instead of sitting on the bed he lay under it, his heart beating uncontrollably faster. He thought about the man on the motorbike. He was frightened. Such people should never be seen anywhere near one's house. They are bad news, he said to himself.

"Riti? Riti? Are you in your room?" He heard his mother's voice. He wanted to reply but then he heard footsteps approaching his door. It was Bianca. She lifted the hem of the dangling bed sheet and saw her brother under the bed, eyes wide open, visibly shaken.

"Thank God, you are back. We saw you sprint out and mother started crying," said Bianca.

"I'm OK, sister. I'll be fine."

"There is a man on a motorbike at the corner there..." Before he could finish his sentence Bianca had quickly walked out. Either she didn't hear or she pretended she didn't.

When Juba finally went quiet after almost forty five minutes of pounding explosion, shaking the ground, injecting fear in the hearts of people, Riti almost dozed off when he heard the sound of a motorbike riding away.

Why did he dash out in the first place? he asked himself.

After a short while Juba was suddenly thrown into spontaneous wailing, crying, shouting and general panic. In the streets women pulled their hair and threw away their cotton fabric wrappers. They shouted the names of their relatives or loved ones. Even men put away their masculinity and joined in the wailing, biting their lips, grinding their teeth in pain or wringing their fingers. Most of the women were running about barefoot. Some of them fainted.

Riti dragged himself from under the bed, dusted himself off and sat on a chair to eavesdrop on people's voices in the street.

"Shelling..."

"Missiles..."

"Long-range..."

"It must be the rebels. The shells were coming from the east..."

Riti heard the shrill voice of a wailing woman who ran into their compound.

"My people, my people, help...help...I'm finished. My aunt Kaku is no more. Dead, she is."

It was Sara's voice. She limply ran into Bianca's chest and the two women tumbled to the ground. Sara sat up and cried, repeatedly slapping her thighs. With tears sliding down her cheeks, she looked like a neglected child.

Riti quickly emerged from his room and walked to where Sara and Bianca were crying. He held Sara's hand but Sara pulled her hand away in anger, her face a flood of tears. Riti squatted to console the two women. He looked deeply concerned. What he gathered from Sara's rapped eulogy was that Kaku, her aunt, who adopted her following her mother's death in Sara's childhood, was dead. Unlike other single mothers of Juba, Kaku had four children, three her own and her elder sister's daughter, Sara, who she had adopted. She was the sole breadwinner and a no-nonsense woman who instilled strict discipline in her children. Her eldest daughter graduated from the

University of Juba the previous year and was now employed as a school teacher in Wau.

With surprise and a sad frown Riti whispered, "What happened?"

"Riti, Riti, my aunt Kaku is dead!" Sara rapped amidst her crying and wailing.

The two women could not be controlled until Riti's mother quietly came and consoled them.

Riti was disturbed. His mind quickly reverted to the man on the black Honda motorbike. Am I safe after all this? He thought.

Kaku, Sara's aunt was cut down by shrapnel. She was cut into bits and pieces. Her intestines and limbs were scattered in the street. Her body parts were collected into cartons and stuffed in a coffin for burial. The manner of her death hurt people very much. Poor Kaku had gone to collect water from a water pump. While carrying a plastic jerrycan on her head a missile lifted her from the ground and scattered her into pieces. The jerrycan was recovered atop a nearby tree, reduced to the size of a mutilated football.

Kaku was buried in the afternoon of the same day. From the cemetery her relatives and friends went to their respective homes, feeling guilty that they couldn't keep vigil with the bereaved family. The state of emergency prohibited the gathering of more than seven people in one place, not even in a funeral party.

Riti and his sister, however, defiantly went out of their way to keep vigil at Kaku's place where Sara had resided until recently. They couldn't abandon her at this dark hour of need, restrictive emergency laws notwithstanding.

That evening when the bereaved family members, including Bianca and Sara, were huddled together to comfort and console each other, a dark-green military jeep parked in front of the gate. Sara craned her neck and got to her feet, as if she was expecting a visitor. A skinny man in military uniform jumped out of the front seat of the jeep and greeted Sara in a guttural Arabic voice. A thick brush of moustache was the most prominent feature on the man's face. The man was trailed by three uniformed men who laboured with a bag of sugar, a bag of charcoal, onions, lentils, a tin of cooking oil, bread. After dropping the items the three uniformed men returned to the jeep to wait for their superior.

The skinny soldier shook the hands of the mourners, saying "Kofara" to condole the bereaved family. He recognised Bianca and exchanged a few words with her.

When the skinny uniformed man drove away with his men, Riti developed goose pimples. He felt as if he had come face to face with Lucifer himself. He then remembered the man on the black Honda motorbike. It was only soldiers and secret agents who roamed in the night in Juba during curfew hours.

A day after Kaku's burial it rained heavily, after the people of Juba had given up hope that it would rain that season. Elders from Kaku's family said the rain was testimony that she was a daughter from a lineage of rainmakers.

◆

The glue that kept the Sudan together as the largest country in Africa was loosening, and it was a matter of time before it disintegrated into two or even more smaller countries. The southern part of the country which identified itself as black was threatening to break away first, after decades of being politically molested by those who were at the centre of power in Khartoum.

Whatever the case, the southerners blamed themselves, especially their ancestors, for their misguided generosity and hospitality, which was the origin of their curse that eventually denied them decent existence in their own country many, many years after.

They traced their curse back to the day a small band of pastoral migrants, all men, who had hailed from the bend of the Nile River, appeared on their land. After the men sojourned for a few months perhaps, and after finding plenty of water and lush grass for their animals, in addition to a pristine environment and the prodigious hospitality of dark-skinned people, they eventually acknowledged that they were truly in the land of the soud or dark-skinned people, and therefore the land they prepared to settle on was indeed Soudan, hence the eponym Sudan.

The migrant pastoralist men who were of light skin and curly hair started going with the local soud girls, and they started having children together, but these migrant men proudly maintained and made their language and way of life superior to the strange ways of their hosts, the dark-skinned people. They even despised their generous hosts.

Hundreds of years of genetic and social engineering produced a hybrid human being who still stubbornly calls himself an Arab, even after he had lost his Arab pedigree. Because he has adopted Arabic as his mother tongue he claims that origin, when in fact he is now referred to as Jallaba by the dark-skinned people. Jallaba might have been a fitting term to describe a peddler, whose ancestors first entered the Sudan as pastoral migrants from the tail end of the Nile River, where grand ancient pyramids stand to this day.

After hundreds of years of enacting the proverbial story of the Arab and the camel, the Jallaba asserted more and more of his birthright on the land, politically edging out the original owner of the land, graphically painting himself in the colours of the proverbial donkey whose vote of thanks is but a kick. The dark-skinned people endured many kicks thereafter. In their own country they are treated as second class citizens with fewer rights, and in due course could be threatened with extinction through ethnic cleansing and a scorched-earth policy. The Jallaba also treated the black people like the tail of a donkey, an appendage that could be cut off or dismembered from the donkey and have no effect on the general health and wellbeing of the animal. The tail was only seen as an accessory for covering the backside of the donkey or for whisking away flies from the donkey's wounds of daily toil.

Mistreatment and cumulative anger became the machine gun for the dark-skinned people to arm themselves with to revolt against Jallaba hegemony. In the first round of the war they made a strong political statement that was loud and clear but didn't succeed, although they had fought a good fight to earn them some rest and regroup for another day. The second round of the insurrection by the people was the one being witnessed firsthand by Riti and his generation. The second civil war was often referred to by the rebels as the mother of all wars to liberate the black people from subjugation and oppression and to restore their dignity, image and self-confidence, eroded by years of political oppression.

◆

The weeks and months that followed the bloody shelling of Juba by the rebels was Juba's darkest chapter autographed by the blood of martyrs. It was a direct assault on the character of the Jallaba. It was like payback time for the camel that was initially ousted from its tent by the selfish northern Sudanese.

The government swiftly went on the offensive by mobilising the army, loyal militia, party stalwarts, sycophants, state machinery and the government-owned media. The media that week unleashed the most venomous of hate speech, calling the inside cells of the rebels 'fifth columnists'.

Then the dogs of war went on a rampage to hunt down the fifth columnists in the suburbs. The highest suspects included mostly university teachers, university student activists, radical and outspoken clergy, intellectuals, civil servants and southern members of the military. Those arrested were immediately booked into the white house for interrogation, systematically tortured, starved, and then they disappeared without trace, except for their names that were engraved in the memories of loved ones who were the silent majority victims in Juba.

Men on black motorbikes loomed large. They roamed the streets like vultures in a battlefield. And whenever one of them was sighted in the neighbourhood it was most likely that a man could be picked up in the middle of the night and whisked away. Some of the secret agents sometimes boasted that whenever the white house was full some of the latest fifth columnists would be tied in sacks and dropped to the bottom of the Nile River to please and fatten the crocodiles and big fish ready for poaching.

That morning, precisely three days after the shelling, Riti arrived in the office unusually early. The janitors had not yet arrived. The old night watchman was about to leave. The dusty office smelled of bat droppings and rotting timber. He was nervous and felt alienated. He was increasingly becoming vulnerable since he saw the man on the black motorbike near their house. He couldn't locate the man's face even in his frequent nightmares. Was he being followed? And why? Riti thought.

There was something eerie about the office environment. He looked through the open window overlooking the airport. The sky was clear. The early morning sun spread her warm wings on the landscape. On the airport runway Riti saw what looked like a military helicopter. His gaze retreated and rested on a patch of land with shrubs and dry grass. This was an open space between the office and the airport. When he was a boy he and his neighbourhood playmates used to frequent the spot to shoot birds with catapults. The birds were either decimated by the boy poachers or have since migrated to the forest when human settlements encroached on the empty space. No wonder the white herons were migrating.

When Riti sat at his desk he noticed that somebody had rummaged through his drawers. Some of the photographs he always kept in the drawers had been dropped on the floor. Maybe his boss was looking for a particular photograph to use in the newspaper? Or was it some malicious colleague who wanted to stir trouble? Riti wondered. He fought hard against thinking that a colleague was up to no good. In order to make peace with himself Riti collected the photographs and put them neatly back into the drawer. He also cleared the drawers of cobwebs and unwanted papers such as back issues of newspapers. He felt lonely. He remembered Sara. Although he longed for a lady's comfort he didn't seem to miss Sara. For the first time he felt as if he didn't love her any more. Something inexplicable seemed to deny him love for Sara. Now he felt like a vulnerable soul walking through a minefield, knowingly.

Riti heard voices downstairs. He composed himself and picked up an old book on photography and pretended to be reading.

"Wow, the early bird is here. Riti, what brings you to the office so early? Got some good photos from ..." said one of the loudest female reporters, as she hugged him as if they had not met in a long time.

Riti said, "I'm planning to go to the airport. The Big Man is coming today." The governor was expected to arrive in Juba that morning after an official visit to Khartoum. As a photojournalist, Riti was to accompany a senior reporter to the airport.

Although he was physically prepared to go to the airport for the press coverage of the Big Man, he was psychologically unprepared. He was nervous. He was traumatised since his last encounter with the skinny man at the airport. The man had warned him against appearing anywhere near the airport. What if they met again even when he was on assignment? When he remembered the experience his eyes narrowed. He was withdrawn. He looked through the window, and beyond, to the soul of things known and unknown. Then, quickly, he made some connection, through a feeling of déjà vu. He could clearly tell that the wiry man at the airport, his nemesis, so to speak, was almost certainly the same man who once dropped Bianca home in a dark-green military jeep, and the same man perhaps who briefly turned up at Kaku's funeral, Sara's late aunt. He told himself that with time he would have to prove his hallucinations.

Presently, the office messenger informed Riti that the boss, the editor, wanted to see him urgently in his office. Being called to the editor's office was often like a pupil being summoned to the headmaster's office for scolding or caning.

The editor's office was spacious, with a large sofa set, deliberately ill-lit and air-conditioned.

The editor sat at his large ebony desk. Behind him on the wall was the president's official photograph in a glass frame. The frozen president was looking down on the editor. The editor's folded hands rested on the desk, in front of him a new black typewriter. He had a bunch of long grey hair that was combed backwards, and an awkward Ho Chi Min goatee. A pair of oval reading glasses perched on the lower bridge of his thin nose, exposing his big white eyes above the rims, giving him a comical look whenever he looked at people. He looked like a colonial officer.

When Riti timidly walked into the spacious office, the editor's widened eyes coldly welcomed him. Riti sensed trouble even before the man could open his mouth.

In his usual soft-spoken but terse voice the editor rolled out his measured words:

"Riti, where are the photographs you took of the woman who was shredded to pieces?"

Riti was taken aback.

"Sir, I didn't take any photos of a shredded woman, I swear by Jesus Christ in heaven."

"Please don't turn my office into a confession booth. All I'm saying is that someone reliably saw you storming out of your house and you were seen around the scene of the carnage, right?"

"Sir, I was actually confused and ran aimlessly like anyone else that morning. But I didn't carry a camera. The office camera is always kept under lock and key in the inventory. The shelling happened before I could come to work."

The editor nodded slowly while staring at the typewriter on his desk.

"Suppose you had a camera, would you have taken such photos after being at the right place at the right time?"

Riti turned the editor's question in his mind and remained open-mouthed.

"Riti, in time of war there is limitation to a reporter's work. Sometimes you have to struggle with moral dilemmas, ethical dilemmas. As a photojournalist, especially, you ask yourself, should I or should I not take such and such a photo, with such and such graphic details? You know what I mean?"

The editor spoke as if he was under pressure from above, which could mean any person perched on the rung above the ladder of authority, or even the frozen face of the president in the glass frame.

◆

A week after the shelling of Juba, which sent shock waves throughout the town, the rebels through their clandestine radio stepped up their media war, this time threatening to shoot down any plane that flew from Khartoum to Juba, alleging that they transported military hardware and weapons, and mercenaries. Despite their blanket threats the rebels should have known that the cargo planes also provided free air transport to southern Sudanese who were travelling from Juba to Khartoum, or from Khartoum to Juba.

Now the regime in Khartoum didn't take the rebels' threats lightly, especially when a cargo plane was narrowly missed by a missile probably shot by the rebels near Malakal.

For almost a month no planes landed in Juba. A Nile barge loaded with essential foodstuffs bound for Juba from Kosti port had the most difficult voyage on the Nile River after coming under heavy gunfire around Malakal and Jemeiza farther south before reaching Juba. The barge took a month to arrive safely in Juba.

Meanwhile, starvation set in. The wholesale and retail shops had run out of food stocks. If there was any little food in the black market the prices were too exorbitant for the ordinary person. The only institutions that still had food in their stores were the army and the state security agents.

The news of the docking of the *MV Jonglei* Nile barge at Juba river port that weekend spread throughout Juba and was greeted with much relief.

The following day Juba residents formed long queues in front of shops that were expected to sell the local staple sorghum, *dura*.

That morning Riti went to a cooperative shop at Rujal-mafi market. He might have been number thirty in the line. The cooperative opened shop to sell its quota of *dura* sorghum by 2pm. By 5pm Riti was lucky to get three buckets of sorghum. Some of the people behind him in the queue were not so lucky. A friend lent a bicycle to Riti to carry the sorghum home.

A few minutes after Riti left the cooperative shop chaos broke out when someone leaked some information that there were more bags of sorghum in a store behind the cooperative shop. The crowd went on a rampage, breaking down the door of the store, and looted the bags of dura that the owners might have wanted to hoard and later sell on the black market. When the police were called in all they found were scattered grains on the dirt ground. But even the scattered dura was later collected by some street families.

Although Riti's mother was grateful for her son's efforts she looked gloomy, pensive, nervous and quite disturbed. Riti couldn't guess what she was going through. He didn't want to ask immediately for fear that it would aggravate matters as she was hypertensive.

He returned his friend's bike and promptly came back home before curfew. He retired to his room shortly after and lay on his bed to listen to the local government-owned radio. A hurricane lamp on a stool dimly lit the room.

"Riti? Riti?" His mother was fond of calling him as if his name carried a question mark. Her tone was very maternal; it reminded him of when she used to call him when he was a boy. From the tone of his mother's voice he could tell that he was called for a meal. When her voice was pampering he knew she had cooked beef stew or chicken stew, but when the tone was flat or sometimes stern he knew it was either vegetables, beans, *pirinda* sauce, or just porridge.

"I'm coming into your room," the old woman announced as she waited outside.

"Come in, Mama."

The old woman slowly entered and sat on the floor despite her son's protestations.

"My son, these old bones are no longer fit for chairs." For some seconds she communicated in silence before she continued, "Son, it is not normal for an old woman like your mother to be coming to her son's room, unless..." she didn't complete her sentence as she suddenly went quiet. Then she began to weep quietly.

"Mama, what is the matter today? Where is Bianca? Is she ok?"

The old woman regained some strength and composure when she said:

"Bianca is in her bar there. She is fine, son. I guess she knows her way back home.

"Riti, my son, when you were in the market, queuing to secure our daily bread, that Sara of yours came here with another Jallaba man who thinks he is the only he-goat in this Atlabara." She paused to run her forefinger on her upper lip to indicate a moustache. It clicked in Riti's mind. He wanted to hear more.

"Then?" Riti prompted.

"Oh, my son, that girl must be dangerous. She must be dangerous." She said these words while shaking her head. "She...or is it they, brought and dropped a bag of grain in the house. It is there." She pointed in the direction of the kitchen without looking there, as if there was something abominable there.

"She boasted that the bag of sorghum was for us because you were seen miserably queuing in the cooperative shop. Oh, oh, my son, your father's house has become a laughing stock indeed.

"Riti, my son, let me ask you candidly. I want you to be frank and honest with me. Is it true that your eyes have admired Sara?" She waited for the reply while looking on the ground, contemplating.

There was prolonged silence in the room.

"My son, you can answer me another day. How about the dura sorghum in the kitchen?"

"Mama, feed the dura to the chickens. Let's not eat it."

"Well, you speak with one voice like your sister. After all, aren't you from the loins of the same man? But I think that Sara is a dangerous girl. I repeat. The way I see her changing men like underwear, she can even infect you with the new disease, oh! Ho! God forbid!"

The old woman said these words and got on her feet, the bones of her joints making the cracking noise of old age.

As she adjusted her dress, she said, "What I have said should remain in this room. Sleep well, my son."

That evening Riti meditated about the importance of having a mother even if you didn't agree with her sometimes. He thought about his relationship with Sara and the dilemma of ditching her at such a critical moment when she was openly being seen in the company of that soldier with a moustache that curls like a hairy caterpillar.

Riti tried to recall how Sara came into his life or how Sara discovered that he had entered her heart. Although love was testing his nerves, he felt some sweet nostalgia. It might have been a year or so ago when she came physically closer to him. It was unplanned. It happened by chance. He was bedridden suffering from malaria. His mother and sister were attending to some urgent family matters somewhere in town. Bianca therefore asked Sara to help nurse him. And she dutifully nursed him very well. He had high fever and was visibly weak. Sara prepared some warm porridge and brought it in a mug to his room. Seeing that he was weak, she timidly sat on the edge of his bed and felt his forehead with the back of her hand. Her hand felt soft and feminine on his head. She smelled nice. He had never been so close to such a sweet smelling human being of the opposite sex.

The scent on her body was like an invitation to a rare feast. Without saying a word Sara dashed out and after a few minutes quickly returned with a wet piece of cloth. She dabbed Riti's forehead with the wet cloth to bring down the high fever. Until then she was Bianca's very close friend but she suddenly became concerned with Riti's health after Bianca entrusted it to her hands that day. She played the good nurse and Riti appreciated her act of kindness.

Riti had not known her very well, but all the same he felt good in her company. He wished she would stay there for him the whole day. He even wished his mother and sister had delayed their return that day. He also wished Sara would not excuse herself to go away to their home.

"Drink the porridge before it gets cold," she said to Riti. "You will feel better." Her words were soothing.

"I'm happy that you came, Sara. Few people are kind-hearted these days in this war-torn Juba of ours," said Riti as a way of compliment.

"This malaria made me very lonely," he continued, trying to strike up a conversation. He looked at the ceiling, although he was stealing weak glances at Sara's slender neck and dark, long hair. Sara didn't seem to sense anything and she didn't say anything.

When Riti finished taking the porridge he started to sweat. Sara then tried to excuse herself. "Let me allow you some quiet rest," she said softly.

"I would prefer you sit here and converse with me. I'm lonely and sick of malaria and loneliness. I'll feel good when I listen to your conversation. You have a nice voice," said Riti, trying to sound miserable.

His bout of malaria was about to blossom into a love story.

That was more than a year ago. But after all that he just heard from his mother, and what he witnessed that evening at Kaku's funeral, he was not sure if there was still some scent left on the page where their love story was written. In two days' time Sara would be celebrating her birthday. Would this be a turning point in their love? He didn't want to think about it. He thought he still loved her but the more he thought about it, the more he seemed to find himself pushed into a love triangle.

◆

Riti loved his narrow bed. It embraced him and gave him refuge from the rude outside world. Since their neighbour Ben disappeared he had been going out less, almost becoming a recluse. He almost stopped hanging out with his buddies. After work he went straight home. His movements have been limited, too. And since Sara harangued him for trying to escape to Khartoum without her knowledge they have been meeting infrequently. Although they mended fences when her aunt Kaku was killed, he felt as if Sara was no longer the same Sara he knew so intimately. He had not found a replacement for Sara because he was not promiscuous and he was not in a hurry, either. Sometimes in his hour of loneliness he wished he had swallowed his pride and met her frequently. He loved her company but he was afraid that Abu-shanab or Mr Moustache might have come between them. When he thought about the army officer with a moustache he tensed up and imagined punching and breaking the man's nose. He breathed heavily as if he really punched the man he imagined to be spoiling Sara's head.

While these wild thoughts zigzagged in his mind somebody quietly slipped into the room. He jumped as if he was found naked.

"Sara! You almost made my heart stop." She giggled and teased, "Don't you have a man's heart?"

She placed a layered meal box on a stool and threw herself on top of Riti. She looked like a thin Japanese wrestler, while under her he looked like an abiding mechanic. She was aggressive. She smothered his lips with hers and kissed him for a long time. She stopped suddenly as if listening to the quiet wind outside. Then they resumed the deep kissing, their clothes falling to the floor and they both looked like intertwined lean trees purged of their leaves by a strong wind. They breathed rapidly and panted in the wrestling match. Sara's perfume enveloped the two of them in a beautiful embrace that left them happy again.

Like characters in a modern Garden of Eden they quickly got into their clothes, deliberately regarded each other with suspicion and burst into laughter as if they had caught some people doing something improper. Their sticky bodies glistened with sweet happiness.

"Tomorrow is my birthday."

"I can't wait for the sun to rise."

"I thought you forgot. Men forget even their own birthdays. Come to our home tomorrow evening. There is a small party."

"How about the curfew?"

"Aren't you a man like those soldiers? Come and dance. You are such a good dancer."

"What type of dance am I good at?"

She understood the joke and quickly gathered the hem of her loose dress and waved it in his face. He inhaled her perfume and was intoxicated with love. He tried to grab her by the waist but she ran out, into space.

Alone, Riti jumped to his feet, energetic, and punched the air with both his clenched fists like a boxer. He pranced around the room as if he had just knocked down an imaginary opponent with a heavy moustache. He replenished the now lost energy by sitting down to relish Sara's excellent cooking, slurping soup and whipping down salad and chunks of spiced pan-fried meats with gusto.

◆

In wartime Juba house parties were prohibited by emergency laws and barred by curfew. Gathering at funerals was also prohibited. Young people only remembered the good old days when house parties were a common feature of social life on weekends. The parties were an excuse for young people to have fun where they engaged in illicit activities like smoking, drinking, and 'quickie' sex that sometimes resulted in teenage girls carrying the burden of unwanted pregnancies.

The parties also offered opportunities for masters of ceremonies (MCs) to show off their public speaking and oratory skills. The MCs pontificated in classical Arabic, occasionally quoting or lifting lines and verses of romantic Arabic poetry by great writers. But after knocking off a few glasses of araqi hard liquor the MCs' tongues would stray back to the bastardised Juba Arabic that they knew better and that they used with impunity to hurl drunken curses at each other.

While civilians were denied partying, the army officers in their mess or club slaughtered goats and soaked themselves in araqi as they partied on weekends. During some national anniversaries or special occasions the army sometimes flew in music bands from Khartoum to entertain them.

Despite being in a war zone the army officers and, of course, the state security agents had fun with good food, booze and women who were not their wives. Most of the officers were northern Sudanese. The local women who consorted with the army officers talked of the lavish lifestyle enjoyed by the officers. Lavish was a relative term as most of the women lived in *tukuls* and were destitute but beautiful and daring enough to frequent the army officers' mess or club on weekends.

The army officers enjoyed their weekend parties for a long time until one rainy August day when the honeymoon ended abruptly. The officers had drunk alcohol, ate goat ribs, danced, and went to sleep with the women of the night. On that rainy night the sleep was so sweet that they didn't hear any outside noise or unusual interruptions. Some daring rebels infiltrated the barracks. They cut the barbed wire fence and gained access to the officers' mess and rooms where they slept with the women. There was no eyewitness to capture the action. When they accomplished their mission the rebels went back to the bush with booty of whiskey bottles, packets of cigarettes, money, and leftover barbecue. Many of the army officers didn't wake up from their sleep.

That incident reinforced the prohibition of house parties in the suburbs. Despite the prohibition and strict observance of curfew, some exclusive parties were thrown in some suburbs. But such parties were heavily attended by armed men in plain clothes.

That afternoon Riti had a haircut. He took a bath and put on some perfume. Smartly dressed, he walked to Sara's birthday. He looked awkward when he found that nothing was happening to indicate a small house party. Sara was smartly dressed all right but the environment looked just normal. Riti bade his time. It was approaching six pm. If nothing happened by seven pm, he would excuse himself to beat the start of curfew at nine pm.

Sara brought a bottle of soda for Riti and whispered something into his ear. He smiled while looking into the distance of Sara's heart. The soda bottle had been opened. It was no ordinary soda, though. It was coke laced with whiskey or vodka, but he couldn't tell the difference because he was not used to exotic drinks. He didn't bother to ask where she got whiskey in wartime Juba.

A number of young people dressed for a party started streaming in and low soft music filtered from one of the tukuls. By now there were about a dozen young people in the compound. Missing was Bianca. Riti preferred it that way so he could 'misbehave' if he chose to when the whiskey caught fire in his head.

This was a foolhardy function held under well-known circumstances, yet any other ordinary person could conclude that this was an act of defiance, if not madness.

The birthday cake was cut in haste in the dark. Then people started drinking and by eight pm, an hour before curfew time, the noise in the compound started to rise. It was clear that most of those who consumed alcohol were literally gulping the contents in a hurry so they could rush home. Cigarette smoke filled the air. Most of the dozen young people almost in pairs were on their feet swaying to the music in the background. Most of them stuck to each other in dance and the girls especially clung to the boys for comfort. Some of the young men started getting out of control, whistling and shouting.

"Increase the volume! Let us dance and die dancing."

Soon the sound of a motorbike was heard outside the fence. The engine was switched off as it parked right in front of the gate. Almost everybody rushed into one of the tukuls. Sara and Riti were the only people left outside. A tall man, presumably the person who was riding the Honda motorbike entered the compound without knocking at the gate.

"Hey, hey, you people, what madness goes on here? Who is here?" said the intruder. Sara approached him and said she was in charge.

"Is this a brothel?" he shouted.

"No. This is a residence. It is the house of our late aunt who was killed on the day of the shelling," Sara said.

"What the hell are you doing? Don't you know that house parties are prohibited?"

"I know, sir."

"What do you know? Where have the cowards gone to hide?"

"They are inside," said Sara with confidence.

"Tell them to march out with their hands raised."

The young people who had taken refuge in the tukul trooped out in single file with their hands on their heads like convicts and a few of them staggered. Meek.

"Lie on your stomachs. Reptiles! And don't move. Don't cough. Don't fart," ordered the tall man.

Addressing Sara, who was now flanked by Riti, the tall man said, "Who gave you permission to hold a party?" Sara didn't say anything but fished out a letter from her bra. The man flashed a cigarette lighter to read the letter which was handwritten in Arabic. He turned the letter over and over before handing it back to Sara, and without a word, he walked out and jumped on his Honda motorbike and sped away.

Riti didn't say a word. He instantly knew that Sara was a powerful lady, probably well-connected. Then Sara asked her guests who were lying on the ground to get up. They dusted themselves off quietly but suppressing laugher. Sara told them to squeeze into the tukul again and continue with life until morning. Boys and girls found fun sleeping together in one room.

◆

Riti's mother dutifully went to church every Sunday except when she was unwell or when she was visiting a sick relative or condoling a bereaved family. Bianca never went to church. She spent Sundays selling beer and counting money in her bar. Riti used to go to church when the security in Juba was a bit better but when the security worsened he decided to spend his Sundays at home, listening to the radio, reading a book or just sleeping all day long.

The following morning after Sara's birthday party, he rolled in bed nursing a stiff hangover. He suffered drumbeats of headache, a bit of melancholy and surreal dreams.

He was alone at home. He enjoyed solitude and the privacy of being left at home alone, although he was a bit apprehensive should a motorbike man intrude into the compound, owing to the fact that the gate did not lock and nobody would know his whereabouts if he disappeared, God forbid. He didn't want to worry about black Honda motorbikes, but thoughts being thoughts he couldn't control some intruding lousy ones.

It was getting humid when he heard footsteps in the compound. He knew it was Sara. He knew her footsteps from the way she dragged her open shoes on the ground. She knocked on Riti's door as if she was up to something suspicious. Riti's eyes looked as if he was still drunk.

"I can see it is still night time in this part of the world," she teased him. "Wake up!" It was unusual that she didn't ask Riti about his mother and sister. Riti somehow presumed that she knew that on Sundays he was the only soul left at home. He heard a motorbike speed by on the main road and he rolled his eyes, but Sara looked indifferent, so maybe the sound of a motorbike only meant something sinister to him and meant nothing to her.

Sara had not drunk liquor but she looked exhausted. She didn't sleep well the previous night. It was her birthday all right, but she had to make sure each and every one who came to her birthday party went back to their home safely. She prayed that nobody would disappear. Now she was happy that it all went well. She slipped off her open shoes and lay near Riti on the bed. Riti was sweating, and the more he sweated the more he smelled of alcohol. Sensing that Sara was quite uncomfortable, or so he presumed, he excused himself to go and have a bath. Sara grabbed his wrist and said, "Sit down! If you want to go to the bathroom I'll escort you. I also want to wash my body." She didn't mean it, but Riti was unwilling to have her escort him to the roofless shelter which was loosely called a bathroom. Riti knew that the bath shelter had no privacy, for it exposed the head and shoulders of a person inside it. He could imagine having a bath together with Sara. What if his mother decided to return early from church, or if Bianca suddenly returned from her bar and found them having a bath? Wouldn't his mother and sister think he was entertaining a prostitute in his late father's house? Wouldn't Bianca in her madness drag Sara out of the shelter and parade her naked in the streets of Atlabara and call her names? Riti thought. The towel round his waist fell off and he didn't pick it up, instead he dived into bed and deliberately rubbed himself on Sara. Her loose dress flew off her shoulders and head, and as if he was possessed by some spirit, Riti was on top of things and started bouncing up and down until the fast beat of Congolese Rhumba music reached the climax.

They were still alone. Naked. Their bodies were sweaty, sticky and exuded a smell that was tolerable, yet tantalising to the senses of the two Sunday sinners.

As soon as Sara left Riti felt weaker and the headache worsened. He decided to have a bath, hoping it would refresh him a bit. When he came out of the bath shelter he saw Leila passing outside the fence.

"Leila, salaam," he greeted. Leila turned and smiled. She parted the bamboo fence to shake Riti's hand. The people of Juba are accustomed to greeting by shaking hands even when the other is eating. Although Leila was headed somewhere in the neighbourhood Riti welcomed her into the compound. Since her husband's disappearance neighbours were supportive and sympathetic to her. She always looked innocent and likeable.

While Leila waited outside Riti entered his room to hurriedly put on clothes.

"Where are Bianca and your mama?"

"Bianca is selling beer and Mama went to church." Riti felt like laughing at the controversy that a beer seller daughter and a devout mother lived under one roof with each minding their own business, and without the other interfering with the other's business.

"Come, we will sit inside the room, it is baking-hot outside," Riti suggested. Leila was reluctant but obliged. Riti avoided mentioning Ben's name to help Leila recover and cope with her grief; after all, neighbours had concluded that Leila's husband had indeed disappeared. Riti and Leila were age mates. When they were younger they used to sing and play the children's games of *boruborut* or hide and seek under bright moonlight skies. Those were memorable days that they always recalled with nostalgia, as their young adult life was accompanied with challenges and headaches of war.

"How's Sara?" Leila asked, as if she had some hidden concern, because after all their love affair was now common knowledge.

"Oh, she just left a short while ago. I thought you met on the way. She is fine. We were at her birthday party yesterday."

Leila stared at Riti with a blank face.

"Do you go to her tea place often?"

"Never. Never. I stopped going there."

Leila continued looking at Riti with a lot of concern. Riti felt it.

"Wise of you. Don't go there again," she said. She sounded authoritative and commanding. "That tea place is a booby trap, if you don't know. Many informers. I'm told a man was stabbed there two weeks ago. Riti, we grew up together in this very Atlabara. We are like children from the same womb." Riti nodded his head slowly, thinking deeply and feeling embarrassed.

Leila lowered her voice and said, "Do you know Abbas?" Her voice betrayed her fear. She sounded paranoid, how couldn't she?

Riti kept quiet for a moment as if searching for an answer. He shook his head thoughtfully and said: "No, I don't know a person by that name. Abbas? No!"

"I don't know him either but I'm told he is a dangerous man," said Leila.

"Who told you?" Riti said.

"You don't want to know." Leila sounded cautious.

Riti imagined many faces that could fit the name Abbas but as he couldn't locate a face he nervously assigned the name to an amorphous face with a thick moustache. Abbas. Abbas. The name registered fear and loathing in his mind.

◆

When Leila left, Riti strolled to a nearby restaurant to have a bite. He was hungry.

When he returned home he went straight to bed. He wanted to nap but ended up staring at the ceiling, turning the name Abbas in his mind. Who is Abbas? What could he be doing or what has he been doing? Dangerous man! He must be a hit man. An informer. Murderer. Killer. Spy. Bloodthirsty vulture. Fundamentalist. Did Abbas abduct Ben and liquidate him in the white house? Is Abbas a hangman? Is he not the man with a black Honda motorbike? Or is he Mr Lover Man, wife snatcher, girlfriend snatcher, widow inheritor? He thinks he has extra testicles? I don't know the man but I feel like puking when I hear his name. I don't want to see Abbas. I hate him with a passion. Abbas, your hands drip with human blood. I spit in your face. Your name is already causing me diarrhoea. Riti's anger reinforced his fear of the unknown.

◆

Sudanese are addicted to spiced sweet tea. The tea is drunk hot in small transparent glasses. The colour of black tea which pronounces the quality of the tea makes it attractive to the sight of the drinker. Men, idle men especially, can drink several cups of sweet tea during the day. Even when there was scarcity of food commodities in Juba tea was not in short supply. Therefore, selling tea was an income earner for some of the streetwise ladies of Juba. They set up makeshift stalls composed of tables and chairs under trees, under shop verandahs or by the roadside. The business thrived mostly at sunset. Tea places also served as social hubs where ordinary folk exchanged and shared day to day life stories. At least this was a small-scale business that was deliberately not prohibited. Some of the tea places were more or less social clubs patronised by regulars.

Tea places pushed a subculture to the urban frontline. It was not about selling and drinking tea that mattered, it was much more to the ordinary business. The ladies who sold tea by the roadside spoke not in Juba Arabic. They spoke fluent refined Arabic which was predominantly spoken by the northern soldiers in the barracks. Their regular customers were soldiers – some of them frequented the same tea places almost daily - as if they had appointments, or as if they were club members who were compelled to show their faces or face penalty. The regular customers sat for a long time conversing, laughing, smoking cigarettes and *shisha* as they drank several glasses of sweet tea. They flashed big denominations, for which they rarely asked for change. The tea girls kept the change. The tea girls largely made their profit from the baksheesh, rather than from the real selling of the tea. But regular baksheesh had strings attached. It was rumoured that some of the tea girls also doubled as night workers, a euphemism for twilight girls. On weekends some of them entertained the army officers in the mess or club, but after that incident when the rebels infiltrated the officers' mess, some of the girls got scared of spending nights in the officers' mess. It was also rumoured that the tea places were clandestine projects set up by the informers so they could trap people with loose tongues.

It was also rumoured that some of the tea girls worked for the state security as informers. The rumour was founded in the fact that the girls were friendly with the uniformed men from the north, to an extent that they shared meals and smoked shisha together. And their conversation and body language was in concert.

The fact that Sara was one of the tea girls made Riti uncomfortable in their love affair. He started questioning and cautioning himself. He wondered if he wasn't a victim of filthy money. If not so, where did Sara get all the money to buy a whole bottle of whiskey on her birthday, if it wasn't given to her by the soldiers? He knew that her daily collection from the tea business wasn't enough to buy a tot, let alone a whole bottle of whiskey. What about the sumptuous food she brought him the other day on the eve of her birthday? Was it only about whiskies and food? What if he was sharing Sara with another invisible man named Abbas? Suppose Abbas the girlfriend snatcher was serially sleeping with twilight girls? What if Abbas infected Sara with HIV which was becoming endemic in Juba?

When Riti thought about these things that night, he got very angry with himself. He was angry with himself for falling in love with Sara. He jumped out of bed and stood in the middle of the room, disturbed. He wanted to scream. He wanted to shout. He wanted to spit. Instead, he grabbed his penis as if to curse the poor thing. While squeezing it he asked himself: "Riti, has this thing of yours infected you with AIDS? When one of your members makes you to commit sin, what do you do with it, but cut it off?" He pinched the tip of his penis until he felt pain in his heart, the very heart which stored the sweet memories of his love for Sara.

He went back to bed. He shed tears of anger. He squeezed the pillow as if he was strangling a human being.

After tossing in bed for some time, he dozed off and even wandered into another world. He saw himself as an outcast rejected by society. He carried on his head a heavy burden of stigma. He was lanky and stooped like a question mark. His eye sockets strained with hollowness. His frame would soon collapse under a pile of sick bones. People in the street avoided him. They fingered him. They ran away from him, all except Sara. Sara was chewing an elixir from a tropical forest. When she kissed him he regained health. He was overweight. He walked with difficulty. He walked for a long time and suddenly fell on Sara's feet. She stood tall like a bamboo. Sara didn't talk to him. She parted her legs and sat on his head. He couldn't breathe. He wanted to cry but his mouth was covered by Sara's backside which smelled like penicillin.

When Riti woke up he was breathing heavily. He was scared. At first he thought he was in a hospital. He had sweated. He had heard that sweating at night was one of the symptoms of HIV. Was he already infected? The more he tried to avoid the thought, the more he thought about it. He shivered.

When he went out to get some fresh air the morning sun was already getting warmer. Bianca looked at him with concern.

"Riti, are you unwell?" Bianca asked.

"I didn't sleep well."

"We heard you screaming in your sleep. Did you have a nightmare?"

"I had a series of nightmares."

"Aren't you late for work?"

"I may not go to work today. I'm not in the mood. Maybe something bad is going to happen to me."

"Take some rest. I'll make for you some light breakfast. Even I'm not feeling well. I'll not go to the bar, the women will help me," Bianca said.

Riti noticed that Bianca had gained weight in the last month or so. He thought she was happy making more money from her bar. Although there was hardship and food was scarce, people were drinking beer to temporarily escape life's problems. With hardship in life and scarcity of food, most people were skinny. It was therefore rumoured that young ladies especially put on artificial weight by orally administering body fattening pills. They thought more flesh on the body would attract them to men. With the money she was making from selling beer, Riti thought Bianca was taking the body fattening pills. But he thought the pills didn't agree with her system because they made her lazy and she was given to sleeping sometimes during the day.

After he took his breakfast, Bianca requested to have a word with her brother.

Bianca rarely had a discussion with her brother, so Riti guessed it was something grave, most probably to do with Sara? He was now open to any suggestion from his family.

Bianca dictated that they discuss in their mother's house where she also lived. Riti noticed that she looked weak. Frail. Her lips were dry. It was as if her pulse was beating faster at the base of her neck.

"Sister, are you alright?" Riti asked.

"I'm fine, Riti, I'm just exhausted. I work hard these days. Some of the women who used to help me in the bar have been poached by competitors. I have no hard feelings, though."

Riti nodded with concern, but he felt as if there was more to what she was saying. Maybe she was under stress. She looked pale. She also seemed to have put on fat around her abdomen like an old sheika. Most owners of beer halls put on weight owing to the fact that they lived a sedentary life. Some of them also gained artificial weight by taking pills. Fatness was associated with success or wealth. The soldiers also loved their women plump. He noticed that of late she and Sara were no longer the best of friends. Something was certainly wrong somewhere.

Lowering her voice, Bianca looked Riti straight in the face and said:

"Do you still want to travel to Khartoum?"

Riti felt ambushed by his sister's question. Was she not the one who told Sara that he had wanted to dump her and escape to Khartoum? Now she was the same person who had turned around offering to help him travel to Khartoum. Maybe it was true that blood is thicker than water, Riti thought.

He moved his head as if nodding and as if he was shaking it.

Bianca was a bit confused but she went on.

"Well, it is about your life. If you want to go to Khartoum I know a friend who can facilitate. He is a soldier, all right, and a northerner, but he can help if I approach him. By the way, all the northerners in the barracks are not our enemies. Some of them sympathise with our people. Some of them are even in the bush with the rebels."

She didn't allow Riti to reply.

"Aha, what about the radio?" she asked.

"Which radio?" Riti was surprised.

"Who doesn't know that you listen to the rebels' radio?"

Riti was nervous. The top of his nose sweated.

"Don't you know that what you are doing is illegal?"

Riti wondered whether his own sister was not a state security agent or informer. He nodded innocently, anger almost clumping in his throat.

Bianca lectured Riti on many issues pertaining to security. All in all, the message was something like: BOY, WATCH YOUR BACK! The message was clearly written on the wall.

That afternoon Riti didn't want to see his radio set again. He had put it away under the bed, out of sight. He had removed the leaking batteries and put them in the sun to dry.

At nightfall he pulled out the radio set and went out and entered the pit latrine with it. And one, two, three...he threw the radio into the dark pit. Swallowed by excrement, forever.

He missed his radio, yet he was happy that he didn't have any incriminating item in his humble abode. The state security agents were welcome any time to search his house, if they suspected him of anything.

◆

That week the MV Jonglei docked at Juba river port.

There was excitement.

The government hyped the arrival of the cargo vessel. The following day journalists who all worked for the only government media were on hand to report about the marine vessel; among them was Riti with an old Russian-made camera to take snapshots of the pyramid of bags piled by the bank of the Nile River.

Sweaty gummayi porters wearing only dirty boxer shorts offloaded hundreds of bags from the MV Jonglei. The porters enjoyed their work. They sang a communal song to make the task at hand lighter. The bags they offloaded seemed lighter. The journalists didn't know what was contained in the bags.

A smartly dressed man who looked like a high-ranking civil servant or a member of the only ruling political party made a curt and casual statement to the journalists. He said something to the effect that the bags of food offloaded from the barge would alleviate the food gap in Juba. Government officials and the media frequently used the term 'food gap' instead of famine.

When Riti left the river port after the government official made the statement, a plainclothes southern Sudanese man tapped his shoulder and said:

"Good work. Did you get good photos of the sacks of dura?"

Riti nodded. "So they were bags of sorghum, eh? I must write that down." He whipped out a piece of paper from his shirt pocket and wrote something to help construct his photo caption. The man, who sounded friendly, boasted to Riti that he was a security man.

For three consecutive days the news about MV Jonglei was in the media and on the lips of people in the local bars.

The residents of Juba were happy.

And for these three days the ordinary citizens in the suburbs milled around the cooperative shops clutching empty bags or holding pails, hoping they would buy some food for their starving families.

◆

A week after the MV Jonglei offloaded her cargo and journeyed back to the north, to Kosti port to be precise, and after raising the hopes of the residents of Juba, it turned out that the hundreds of bags were not sorghum. There was anxiety and utter disappointment when the residents learned that the bags contained seeds of watermelon, locally known as *tisale*. Southern Sudanese were not known for planting watermelon. Due to ignorance there were myths surrounding some agricultural products coming from the north. These myths were manufactured by economic saboteurs who didn't like southerners to venture into diversified agriculture. It was said, for instance, that onions couldn't grow well in the south because they required waste matter excreted by bedouins. Many Southerners believed the narrative.

So throughout the country watermelon seeds could not be called snacks. They were just seeds. They were soaked in salty water and dry-fried in a pan. The fried seeds were shelled with the teeth, making a cracking sound which required expertise. The inner, soft seed would be chewed, but not eaten as food. *Tisale* look like pumpkin seeds but are smaller in size. Young people cracked *tisale* as they watched a soap opera on TV, sat in the cinema or at a football match, to pass time the way popcorn is popular with cinema or theatre-goers in some countries.

Because *tisale* was not solid food, the product was hard to sell the week the cargo barge arrived in Juba. It was the ingenious women of Juba who turned *tisale* into a delicious vegetable ingredient. Until then the people of Juba got used to eating their greens without the rare peanut butter seasoning. It took one woman to un-shell a handful of *tisale* which she ground to a paste and marinated with some vegetables that tasted like *simsim* paste or *basiko* traditional dish. Soon the bags of *tisale* sold out like hot cakes.

The merchants who shipped the watermelon seeds to Juba in time of war and hunger might have cursed their miscalculated assumptions. Their ulterior motives had failed. They were exposed.

Although *tisale* became a favourite ingredient in the cooking of vegetables to make the traditional *basiko* dish, Riti was angry with himself for misleading his people when his photo caption in *Juba Times* weekly newspaper mentioned that the *MV Jonglei* had brought hundreds of bags of sorghum. He had to get used to the fact that in times of war propaganda and blatant lies were the staple of government-owned media as independent newspapers did not exist then, they could not exist, they were not allowed to exist, or to counter the government propaganda machine.

He wanted to resign from work as a photojournalist to extricate himself from the so-called collective responsibility but he didn't know what else he would do if he chose to resign. He didn't have any plan B. He had no university education and it meant that with his school certificate and a lean CV he would have to walk the streets of Juba for months or years in search of a white-collar job. If he were to face such difficulties in life he wouldn't depend on his sister, who was increasingly behaving as if she was a state security agent intern. However, he convinced himself that if the worst were to happen he would be forced to hew firewood, burn charcoal, or sell Nile River water for a living.

Some days when he considered resigning from work he thought of making his last attempt to fly to Khartoum, hoping Bianca would enlist the assistance of her amorphous northern Sudanese friend. But when he remembered his last encounter with Mr Bad News at the Juba airport lounge he refused to entertain the idea of going to Khartoum. His fear was compounded by his frequent bumping into the state security agent he met at Juba river port when the *MV Jonglei* docked with a cargo of *tisale*.

He felt that he was seriously being stalked by invisible people. After throwing his radio into the shithole he felt he was a clean citizen. Or was he not?

◆

In his wildest moments of sub-consciousness Riti had concluded that Sara was the invisible person stalking him. He imagined her following him in the streets, standing behind his desk in the office, and silently mocking him when he visited the pit latrine or in his sleep.

He had not seen her in days and he didn't miss her, after all he was convinced that she was the invisible person stalking him. What did she want from him? What was she up to? He was looking for her physically. He went to their place. She was not there. He went to the marketplace. She was not there. He went to her tea place. She was not there either. Nobody knew her whereabouts. Nobody cared. Maybe she was in the army barracks to be infected with gonorrhoea? When he thought that she was hiding from him as a permanent invisible person he bumped into her in a pharmacy at Malakia. When she saw him, she wanted to run away to mutate into an invisible person, but he grabbed her by the wrist and dragged her into a large, one-roomed house. He pinned her against a double-decker metal bed. She wanted to scream but she lost her voice. Her long hair was dishevelled. Her eyes popped out as if she was choking, dying. She had no shoes on her feet. She had no clothes on. He continued to pin her onto the metal bed and forced his weight on her. She didn't look like someone he knew. She was a stranger. He wanted to plant a kiss on her angry lips. But she had no lips. As he struggled with her he saw his body being dismembered. His severed right foot floated above his head. His intestines hung from a rusty fan like clothes drying on a line. His body parts were stuck against the high ceiling. She watched in amazing revenge. He wanted to scream but he couldn't, his mouth remained open. When he opened his eyes he was bathed in sweat and breathing heavily.

When he woke up he was excited to find himself in his room in Atlabara. His boxer shorts were a mess of okra syrup between his legs.

"Shit!" he shouted.

Harsh rays of the morning sun intruded into his room. He was disturbed by what seemed like a real life experience.

He sat on a rock outside his room to soak in the morning sun. The rock was warm under his buttocks.

He cupped his head between his hands, still disturbed. He wanted to decipher the meaning of that disturbing dream. Was Sara trying to sacrifice him?

"Riti, are you alright?" his mother asked. She dropped the broom she was sweeping the compound with and shuffled to where her son sat. Riti looked thinner.

"I just had a bad dream, Mama. I've never dreamed like this in my life."

"What did you dream about?" Riti's mother prompted. "I hope it was not someone trying to bewitch you last night. The war has displaced all the village witches to Juba. In fact, Bianca and I heard you scream in your sleep like someone being choked."

Riti could not narrate the graphic details of his dream to his mother.

"I dreamt that I was drowning in a river full of crocodiles," he lied. Morally he could not find himself telling his mother that he dreamt that he was raping his Sara in an asylum and then an invisible hand castrated him.

◆

Riti seldom went to church. Before Ben's disappearance he used to hang out with the boys at the club to play dominoes and whist. The previous night's nightmare scared him and he wanted some divine help. He went to St Theresa Cathedral for the general Sunday mass. As a baby he was baptised in the same cathedral. To the people of Juba the cathedral was a safe haven in time of war. During the first civil war in the 1960s and more at the height of the 1965 Juba massacre many civilians sought refuge under the large arms of God in the cathedral. Just a couple of months ago when Juba was shelled by the rebels many people ran to hide in the fortified church. While many young people of his age dressed to kill when they went to church, Riti was casually dressed as if he was going to fish. He wore a white t-shirt, a pair of worn out khaki trousers and a pair of *mutukeli* sandals locally made from old car tyres. But more significant to him was a blue-beaded rosary which dangled from his neck like a noose. He looked more like an altar boy than a young photojournalist.

He sat in the middle ebony pews near the isle. Where he sat was a vintage point to see the clergy conduct the mass. Sometimes his mind strayed to the Christian murals with African motifs on the wall or the high ceiling. The murals humbled him. He truly felt he was in a hallowed citadel. When he was not looking at the murals or the altar he studied the heads of the worshippers. Most of the men's heads had dusty, kinky short hair, with a few balding heads with greying hair. Most of the women had their hair plaited in beautiful parallel rows, while a few others had their hair plaited vertically and the pointed ends jutted upwards like nails; this fancy style was called Congo-Congo. Riti wondered how women with such style went to bed without spoiling their hair and worse, if such women picked a street fight. A few elderly women tied their heads with white scarves.

During Holy Communion Riti didn't partake. He remained seated in the pew as he watched worshippers walk past him in a neat line along the isle to take communion. The worshippers looked meek, some of them pretended. His eyes landed on the back of a tallish young lady in a green flowery dress. His heart beat faster as he craned his neck to see the face of the lady whose shoulders looked familiar. When the lady took the communion she didn't return through the aisle. When Riti recognised the lady as Sara he dropped his gaze and pretended to be meek also. He clutched his rosary and mumbled something. Maybe what he mumbled was meaningless. Pure gibberish.

After mass Sara disappeared into the crowd and into thin air.

In the cathedral compound Riti walked among the worshippers who were hugging, pumping hands, conversing and laughing despite problems visited on them by the war. He couldn't see Sara. He greeted a few people he knew and walked away. Although he felt he didn't want to see Sara, he felt hurt at the same time. Didn't she see him? Did she give him the cold shoulder? Did she have a date with another man?

While Riti wandered in the jungle of his head he felt inadequate. He felt something was lacking in him. He felt deprived. Of love. Of happiness. And the more he felt vulnerable.

Riti walked back home, avoiding shortcuts, to take the two kilometre dusty Chief Tombura Road. The sun was overhead and the sand was roasting beneath his feet. A sudden dry, early December wind blew in his direction, lifting her wings and licking Riti's face with a wave of heat, dust and particles. He wished he could go to the club to play dominoes, have a chat with the boys and drink hot, sweet tea.

When he arrived home he found the door of his room wide open. He remembered very well that he had shut the door and even padlocked it. The door of his mother's house was locked. He stood in the compound, perplexed.

"Bianca, Bianca, is it you in my room?" Riti called.

There was no answer.

"Bianca?"

It was all quiet.

Slowly, he shuffled towards his room. He told himself 'come what may' and entered the room.

He couldn't believe himself.

His mattress was thrown on the floor. His clothes were piled on the mattress. A small carton with his personal belongings was emptied onto the mattress as well. He looked around the room but apart from the deliberate mess and chaos, nothing was stolen. He couldn't suspect the person or people who broke into his room although his fears were heightened. He finally concluded that the person who intruded into his room was searching for something particular, which they didn't find. And because they failed in their mission they messed up the room as if to say 'we will get you'. Who were they? What were they looking for? Suppose they had found his radio?

Riti had not seen the man on the black Honda motorbike in a while. Could he and his cohorts be the ones firing the warning shots?

"God is in control." Riti whispered the words to the wind, hoping the invisible trespassers could hear him.

He went to his mother's kitchen, his steps heavy with fear and anxiety. He sat on the dirt floor of the kitchen and his eyes exploded into bitter tears. Tears of anger. He folded his right hand into a fist and punched his open left hand as if he sought revenge. When he recovered his composure he wiped the tears from his cheek and blew his nose into a crumpled rag that smelled like a baby's vomit. He got up and stood on his feet. With hands akimbo, he spat on the dirt floor, his eyes full of anger and contempt. Outside the compound a notorious dry season billy goat on heat was chasing a nanny goat, bleating and puffing, wanting to mount. Riti smiled. He was listening to the goats and wanted to know if the billy goat would succeed. Then he remembered Sara. The green flowery dress. The cathedral. Holy Communion. Holy Spirit. He went to pee because he didn't have anything to do, or he didn't know what to do. He was confused. It was as if he was under house arrest. He was only connected to the outer world by the sounds of children giggling, a bicycle bell, the shout of a passing charcoal vender on a donkey, and the donkey farting and dropping wet cakes of dark green dung.

◆

On Monday morning Riti arrived in the office like on any other day. He went to the canteen to drink a cup of tea and to eat a snack. He knew that day that he would have to wait until evening before he could eat a major meal. Times were hard, people ate only once a day, but some people were not so lucky, they starved.

It was a lazy day, typical of Mondays. Today he wasn't assigned to cover a news story. It was what news reporters call a dry day. Some days in Juba passed unnoticed with insignificant news. News was all about Big Men telling lies, making empty promises and talking war as if they were the ones actively fighting in the battlefield.

On days that he was not assigned a story to cover Riti would sling the office camera around his neck like a big necklace and track the main streets, hoping to chance on a human interest story or street drama.

At around noon Riti found himself alone in the office, except for the clerks, cleaners, and the bookish editor. He decided against going out, preferring to remain in the office to read a book on photography. The office was stuffy and humid. He was bored. He almost dozed. He got up and walked to the Gothic window. He was greeted with hot air. He had a telescopic view of the airport. In December the grass was dry. During the dry season people who lived on the outskirts of the town burned the dry grass. Riti could see patches of burned fields west of the airport. He loved the landscape in the wet season when it was lush and green and the birds sung beautifully.

He went back to his desk and continued reading the book on photography. He admired some of the techniques used in black and white photography and he wanted to experiment with them one day.

A few hours later Riti heard a raspy knock on the door. Two heavily built men entered the office and found Riti at his desk, rubbing his chin which was beginning to sprout hair. Due to the general acute food shortage most people in town were skinny but the two strangers looked well fed and healthy, an indication that they were new arrivals, most probably from Khartoum.

"Riti, how are you?" said one of the two men. He sounded friendly as if he knew Riti. Although Riti was quite surprised he didn't show it. The other man wore an expressionless face.

"You are the photographer here, aren't you?"

Riti nodded. He didn't know the two strangers. He couldn't remember meeting or seeing them. He could swear he didn't know them. They were southerners, alright, but they spoke in fluent, refined Arabic. They spoke like people who had studied in good Arabic schools in northern Sudan.

"We are security. We are on duty. Can you get away from your desk for a minute?" The man said this while his colleague remained silent.

Riti obliged.

One of the security men, the one who didn't say a word at all, went to Riti's desk and pulled open the drawer. He rummaged through black and white printed photographs. He shuffled the photographs like cards and stopped to study a photograph that caught his attention. He twisted his mouth sideways and spoke for the first time.

"Riti, you have such a rich photo library. Were you the one who took all these photos?" The man's voice sounded feminine, which didn't match his masculine physique.

Riti sort of nodded innocently. He never locked his drawers because it was a public office.

"We found what we are looking for. Can you accompany us to headquarters?" said the security man with the feminine voice.

Riti hesitated, confused, but managed to say, "My boss must know where I'm accompanying you to because I'm still on duty."

"Your boss will know eventually," said the man with the feminine voice.

Riti's eyes swept the walls of the office as if to say goodbye, and he followed the security men outside to a waiting white jeep pickup vehicle covered with canvas. There were two other men in the vehicle, bringing the number to four security men.

"Get into the car, boy, it won't take long," said the security man.

People in the compound of *Juba Times* didn't notice anything suspicious. The atmosphere was peaceful when the jeep pulled out of the gate. The two bulky men at the back of the vehicle grabbed Riti by the neck and forced him to lie face down. One of the men stepped on his head with a heavy boot which smelled of fresh excrement.

Riti cried silently. He didn't know where he was being taken and why he was being manhandled. He didn't know if his mother and sister would see him again. He never thought or remembered about Sara.

The men in the car didn't say anything as if they were strangers to each other, although the driver knew where he was heading. The jeep drove off, cut sharp corners and appeared to travel for a long distance although Riti could tell from the familiar sounds that they were still within Juba. He heard a match being struck, and shortly a strong smell of marijuana filled the interior of the jeep. After driving for almost forty minutes the car suddenly stopped. Dust rose. Riti choked under the heavy boot. The boot slowly lifted from his head. Riti remained lying down, his face a smudge of tears and dust, the smell of fresh excrement rubbed on his face. His eyes were shut tight. He waited to be told what to do, or so he thought. With both eyes shut he could tell he was in a military barracks or thereabouts. A distant voice shouted drill orders. He heard boots grinding on stones. All he could hear were either commands, swear words, or a hand slapping a rifle. He also heard the grating sound of a metal gate closing or opening. It was humid.

Around him in the car all was quiet, but when he slowly opened one eye, he saw one of the security men staring at him with bloodshot eyes. Riti quickly shut his eyes and continued to flood his face with tears.

He lay in the car for about an hour or so with little movement. He wanted to pee. Soon he heard a strange voice.

"Riti, get down quickly." When Riti opened his eyes to alight he saw a different man. He didn't know where the other security men had disappeared to. The man wore a dark safari suit, his small sized feet were in slip-on crocodile leather shoes, a stick of cigarette was sandwiched between his thin, dry lips. He blinked at quick intervals like a stammerer.

Riti was surprised to learn that he was actually in the premises of the high court, which was about two kilometres from his workplace. It was four o'clock in the evening and government offices had closed.

"Follow me," the man said calmly. They entered the basement. It was almost dark in the room, which was a makeshift cell. There was only one wooden chair in the room. The man sat on it and crossed his legs. He said to Riti, "Sit down". Riti looked around the room with searching eyes.

"I said sit down," the man, who was obviously a state security agent, said politely but with authority. Riti found himself sitting on the floor in a powder of dust and grains of sand. For fifteen minutes the man looked at Riti without opening his mouth but his eyes said many things that scared Riti. The man lit another stick of cigarette and puffed slowly, thoughtfully, as if waiting for someone or something to prompt him to talk or act. The cell was now filled with smoke. Riti coughed. He could not think properly because he didn't know why he was being treated like a suspect or thief.

"What is your name?" the man asked.

"Riti."

"Where do you work?"

"*Juba Times* weekly newspaper."

"Are you a sweeper, messenger, or watchman?"

"I'm a photo-journalist, sir. I take pictures of government officials. Important people."

"What else do you do? Or, put it this way. Who else do you work for?"

"I only work for the government." Riti now wanted to pee, badly. "Sir, I would like to go for a short call."

The man looked at Riti and said: "Urinate. In your pocket."

Riti bit his lower lip but he could not hold his bladder any more. The warm, smelly liquid from his body soaked his trousers. He was ashamed but relieved. He stared at the floor. The urine made a map around him on the floor.

The man reached for his shirt pocket as if to fish out a packet of cigarettes. He took out a coloured photo and raised it to Riti, whose eyes were downcast.

"Do you know the man in this photo?"

Riti looked up and studied the photo and shook his head.

"I put it to you. I repeat. Do you know the man in the photo?" the man insisted. Riti shook his head.

"If you don't know the man in the photo then you are not fit to be a photographer in a government newspaper."

The man walked out. Riti thought about his mother and sister who would not know his whereabouts. If he didn't return home that evening they would conclude that he too had been snatched and taken to the white house like Ben. They will not sleep. They will weep the whole night or maybe weeks to come. They will keep vigil.

Riti heard a car being started and driven off. It was getting darker in the basement cell. Soon he heard footsteps. He saw the silhouette of two tall figures with things that dangled from their hands like river snakes. The men locked the door and switched on the light, and without saying anything, they started beating him with hippo hide whips. They whipped him on the head, hands and back and when he rolled on the floor, writhing in pain and yelling, they kicked his buttocks and ribs hard. They whipped him for about ten minutes nonstop without feeling anything even as Riti cried for mercy. Riti heaped his hands on his head to protect his eyes, nose and ears from being hurt. The two tall men beat up their victim until he went limp like a rope. They were sweating when they stopped. They were tired of beating their victim.

"Idiot! That is the early supper we give to rebel collaborators. Rebel. Cassava thief," one of the men shouted even when, from experience, he knew that the victim he was addressing couldn't hear him.

The men walked out with their chests extended, heaving with ego. They sweated. Their shirts were soaked as if water was poured on their backs.

At midnight Riti started to snore with laboured breaths. He yelled: "Sara, Sara, don't kill me...don't..."

At dawn Riti stirred and groaned in pain. The floor of the cell was cold. He turned but felt pain all over his body. He also felt pain in his bones. He hissed. His eyes were still shut. He mumbled as if complaining, maybe of the pain. At a distance roosters crowed, dogs barked and donkeys brayed. He opened his eyes and felt a bitter sensation. He had difficulty opening his eyes fully. He blinked. He coughed and spat. He didn't know where he was. He was confused.

"Where am I? This is not my bed. It is hard. This house smells strange, eh?" He whispered. He threw out his legs and arms and they hit the dusty floor hard. He winced. His body was dusty and sandy.

"Who brought me to the roadside? Ah, iiihh, I'm hungry. I have a headache. Oh, my ribs are broken. Hold my head."

At sunrise after he came to his senses he sat up and leaned against the smudgy wall. He looked at the open door. His eyelids were swollen. He strained his eyes to see well. His lips were swollen. The bodily pain was unbearable.

He could see the orange rays of the morning sun. Birds were chirping on top of neem trees in the compound. Somebody was whistling a tune outside. The man who was whistling approached the door of the cell and shouted:

"You, fifth columnist, get out!"

Riti struggled to his feet as if confirming the man's assertions. He felt as if his ribs were broken. He walked with unsteady steps. He walked as if he was stepping on hot coals. He had no shoes on his feet. He gnashed his teeth. He smelled of stale urine. Before he could gain his balance two pairs of hands swept him off the ground and hauled him into a military jeep and blindfolded him. He was pushed onto the floor of the car. There was a nasty smell of rot in the jeep.

The jeep zoomed off.

Riti felt as if his whole body was swollen. There were welts on his skin. His ribs ached whenever the car hit a pothole. The car seemed to travel on a straight road up to a certain point when it slowed and turned left. It appeared to slope downwards before it started to climb a steep road, then slowed down and stopped abruptly with a jerk. He heard boots jump down on what sounded like gravel.

It was windy and chilly. His ribs ached. He felt filthy, thirsty and hungry. He hated what he was going through. "Why me?" he thought.

Still blindfolded, some hands pulled him out of the jeep and he landed on the gravel with his feet. The sharp stones cut into his bare feet. He felt the stinging pain deep in his heart like some crude vibration.

He was walked into a metal cargo container. The interior of the container smelled of stale sweat, the cannabis mash bhang, dry shit, urine and rot of ages.

The container was semi-dark with rusty walls. There was spittle and cigarette ash and butts on the floor.

The blind was removed from Riti's eyes and he saw three uniformed men, all armed with pistols. If Riti's mother was to be brought to the container at that moment she would swear by her withered breasts that the young man with a swollen face was not her son.

Riti's legs were unsteady. He was shivering. He was scared. He was hungry. He was weak. He was worried. He smelled as if a bucket of urine was thrown at him. "Did you take a bath yesterday?" One of the uniformed men who looked as if he was senior to the other two addressed Riti.

Riti shook his head.

"Remove your clothes," said the man. Riti hesitated, but when the other two soldiers came closer to him with blazing eyes he removed his crumpled shirt and the urine stained trousers. He was now in his underwear.

"What are you still waiting for?" the man asked. "Why did you wet yourself? Are you a baby? This place will make you a man or woman if you choose." Riti obliged.

He was now a naked man in front of three uniformed men. He didn't know what was going to follow. He didn't have the energy and tears to cry. The only man who was giving commands to Riti gestured with his head and his two lieutenants saluted and left the container. Shortly, another uniformed man, short and lean, entered with an empty big bottle with a long neck. He handed Riti the bottle. "For you to piss," said the man who had been giving orders.

Riti turned his back to the two men and squeezed into the bottle some drops of dark yellow urine. He was dehydrated. He was shivering from fear.

"Put the bottle down."

The soldier who had brought the bottle exited. Shortly, four uniformed men entered. The only man who remained in the container throughout to give verbal orders said, "Riti," pronouncing the name with a northern accent. "We don't have chairs for our visitors. But feel at home. This is your new home. Now, sit on the bottle. That is your royal stool. Sit!"

Riti was confused. How could he sit on a standing bottle with a long neck? He thought he could place the bottle on its side, but the four uniformed men threatened him with their eyes, their right hands caressing their pistols.

"Sit on the bottle, I say."

Riti bent in his nakedness and before he knew it the four men had forced him to sit on the bottle. The bottle penetrated his anus. He broke into tears, his eyes wide bulbs, and his teeth gnashed.

"Stand up!" the man shouted.

Riti got up with difficulty as his body ached a lot. When he stood upright the bottle was stuck in his anus as if he had a hard tail. The uniformed men laughed, except for the one who was giving orders.

"Face the wall."

When Riti turned around, the bottle still dangling from his backside, one of the uniformed men kicked the bottle with his boots and it dropped to the floor but didn't break.

Riti tumbled onto his stomach. He breathed but his limbs were limp.

He woke up when the unbearable heat in the container started to roast his naked body. He was alone, or so it seemed. It was dark. He couldn't tell the time. He was resigned to the pain. He was resigned to fate. If there was an end to his torture he wanted it to happen very quickly. He groped for his clothes and struggled to get into them. The heat was suffocating. The container was filled with a foul odor. He felt a stinging pain in his anus. It was as if his entrails had been turned inside out. He breathed with difficulty. A notorious thought told Riti to try the door of the container, and if it was not locked he should escape. He, however, decided against the thought for fear of risking being shot. He put his right hand in his trouser pocket and felt his rosary. He removed it and kissed it three times and said a Hail Mary. Then he put the rosary back in his pocket.

He fell asleep for what seemed a long time. He was woken up by a pack of dogs fighting near the container. He heard a bugle being blown, and the crowing of roosters at a distance. This only meant that the suburbs were a bit far from where he was being held. He guessed he was within the vicinity of the white house. If this was the so-called white house why was he being kept in a container, alone? He doubted it. He could hear people outside the container but couldn't pick up what they were saying.

It was the third day of his detention without any charge being read to him. He was being detained by the army or state security agents, not the police. There was a state of emergency in the country. The state security agents arbitrarily arrested and detained people they suspected of being a threat to national security. Riti didn't know how he could be a threat to national security when he only used a camera to shoot people. Others used the gun.

While his mind was having a dozen disconnected thoughts he heard a clanging noise and the door of the container creaked open. Some fresh air entered the container momentarily, flushing out the foul smell.

A slender uniformed man entered gingerly as if he was afraid of stepping on a fresh piece of shit. He had curly hair and a heap of a moustache that covered his upper lip. He had baggy eyelids as if he didn't have enough sleep. He stood near the door and with his index finger he motioned to Riti to draw closer. The man was smoking a thin roll of marijuana. He looked at Riti but Riti's eyes were staring at the man's boots. The left boot had stains of blood.

"What is your name?"

"Riti."

"Who brought you here? Why are you here? What did you do?"

Riti kept quiet and the man didn't press him. Riti plucked some courage from his reserve energy to look the man straight in the face and said, "Are you Abbas?"

The man frowned, surprised.

"Do you know me?" the uniformed man asked, as a knowing smile lingered.

"My sister is Bianca. We stay in Atlabara. I'm innocent."

The man dropped the butt of what he was smoking, stepped on it with his right boot and ground it like an insect.

"Bianca is in hospital," the man said calmly and walked out.

Riti had only feared for his hypertensive mother. He was afraid her blood pressure would give her problems since he went missing. But he didn't know what might have happened to his only sibling, and literally the breadwinner. He became nervous.

The man with the bushy moustache returned with a glass of hot sweet tea.

"Fadhal, drink some tea, it is halal tea," the man said. Riti's hands shook as he put the glass to his lips. After a while his body exploded into sweat. He felt sticky in his armpits and groin.

The uniformed man took the empty glass and walked out. He delayed for about ten minutes. It was a quiet Thursday morning. Riti faintly heard the beautiful singing of birds. He longed for the freedom the birds enjoyed.

The man entered quietly with a pair of slippers and handed them to Riti. He didn't throw them at him.

"Wear those," he said.

Riti was happy to put his aching feet in the slippers. He felt as if his toenails had been removed. The slippers were oversize. Maybe the slippers belonged to a departed soul. Maybe they belonged to Ben? he thought. If they were going to kill me why were they bothering to give me earthly things to wear? He looked at the man and solemnly said, "Thank you." The man was touched. He went out without saying a word. Maybe he went to wipe a tear out of sight, for even soldiers weep.

When the man returned he told Riti, "Time to move on." Riti went cold. He thought he was being taken to the gallows or to be shot dead.

The morning sun blinded his eyes. He blinked and shielded his eye with his left palm. The man walked to a jeep, opened the door of the passenger seat and with his hand politely motioned to Riti to enter. The man sat on the driver's seat, inserted the ignition key and turned it on. The car coughed to life with a jerk. They were the only two in the car.

When the jeep gathered speed, Riti could now tell with a clear vision that he was indeed detained in the military barracks. The white house.

"My name is Abbas." The man introduced himself and never said anything else until the jeep entered the main gate of the Juba University teaching hospital. He dropped Riti there and said, "Greet your sister."

Riti felt like an outsider. He looked at his feet with shame. The slippers were not only oversize, but they were of different colours and for the same foot. With his swollen face, uncombed hair, repugnant body odour and crumpled and stained clothes, he looked like a thief who was beaten by a street mob. He sat on a slab and pondered who to start asking where his sister was, if she was indeed admitted in a ward. Besides, he reasoned that the nature of illness will determine the ward number. He only knew the casualty ward and Ward six for tuberculosis patients. As a press photographer he had done some work in these wards. A young woman in a toub wrapper walked past him to catch a bus.

"Leila," Riti called with a weak voice. The young woman turned but didn't bother to look at the man with the swollen face and dirty, crumpled clothes.

"Leila, it is me, Riti, you can't recongise me?" Leila, the neighbour whose husband, Ben, had disappeared almost seven months ago covered her open mouth with her palm. Her eyes were wide open in disbelief. She ran to Riti and embraced him, sobbing. Her stomach was swollen. She held his hand and pulled him back in the direction of the wards from where she had come. They did not say anything until they neared a ward. She whispered to him as if it were a top secret: "Sara went to Khartoum two days ago. She eloped with a northern soldier. Can you imagine!"

The two entered a ward with women occupying the beds. Some of the women were nursing newborn babies. Riti's eyes fell on his mother sitting on a bed at the far end of the ward. Newly born babies were crying. Nurses pushed trolleys of food. His mother didn't recognise him at first.

"Mama, Riti is alive," Leila announced as if to the whole ward. His mother jumped to her feet. She raised her hands and wailed. She embraced her son and they both cried on each other's chests. She dragged him to the bed where Bianca was lying near a newborn baby. Bianca burst into tears. She couldn't get up. Riti embraced his sister for a long time, crying. They hushed what they wanted to express. Riti's mother raised her hands to thank God for bringing her son back alive from the lion's den.

Riti's mother pointed at the newborn baby who Bianca was breast-feeding and said, "Riti, see your little nephew. He came into the world yesterday evening." Her voice lacked enthusiasm or happiness.

The baby had very light skin, almost white. His dark, curly hair was pasted on its small head. He had large ears, Riti noticed, and nodded thoughtfully. He held the baby's little fingers and wept. With all the streams of silent tears he was able to laugh at the little bundle on the bed being nursed by his sister.

Riti excused himself and went outside as he was conscious of his filthiness. He sat on the grass under a *neem* tree. He wanted to take a bath and change into clean clothes and shoes. Alone, he didn't feel safe. Leila joined him and there was pity in her eyes. "I'm happy to see you alive, Riti. Yours is a long story for another day in times of happiness and peace," Leila said softly, her words comforting and reassuring. Riti felt himself as the odd man out, filthy and battered. His face was not only swollen from the beating and torture, but also from the humiliation. He was pushed against the wall of the world. He was bitter, unforgiving, unrelenting. He blamed himself for the reck-lessness. It was that mislaid photograph of his icon, the rebel leader, which almost claimed his life. He convinced himself that had the oppressive system killed him he would have died a martyr. His name would have been etched in the history pages of the liberation struggle as a freedom fighter. He secretly worked for the rebels; he was what was called 'internal cell'. He relayed valuable information such as the movement of military convoys out of Juba to the battlefield. He also reported on military casualties during the shelling of Juba. He vowed to fight the system from within. In only four days his eyes had sunk into their sockets. He was emaciated, weak, hungry and angry.

His mother brought him some warm porridge and avoided looking at him directly. She bit her lower lip to avoid crying in public.

Riti ate the porridge slowly, thoughtfully. His mind was occupied with plans for his immediate future now that he had escaped the dungeon where few people escaped alive. It was because of Bianca's affair with Abbas that he was able to come out alive. So Bianca was sleeping with the enemy. He thought. She slept with the enemy and carried the enemy's seed in her womb for nine months. Did Abbas rape her? Who will buy that crap? Now she has Abbas junior who will forever keep the history of oppression alive in their family memory. He doesn't want to be reminded of that ugly history every day.

Riti's mother asked, "Leila, my daughter, can you please go and check on your sister, Bianca? I'll come soon."

Riti's mother turned to Riti without looking in his eyes and talked to him in a low tone:

"My son, whether it was Abbas or God, but no, it was God who saved you from death, let's praise God. Abbas is an exploiter, a murderer. See what he has done. I'm not happy at all with Abbas and Bianca. She has brought a curse to this house. She has been going with a man who is a killer of our people, and that is a curse. All along I have been hoping against hope that she would marry the son of Bonkir. Bonkir is one of us. His family is known for purity. All these years I have been in this Juba I have never heard that the Bonkirs are murderers, witches; they don't even possess snake poison. They are a respected family.

"Riti, the evil people who wanted you dead are still at large. They may be planning to kill you. I don't know their motive. So, be extra careful. Watch your back. Movements..." Before she could finish what she was saying to Riti, they saw Abbas coming towards them. He greeted them and said he was taking Bianca home.

When Abbas entered the ward Riti's mother spat with spite.

"Let him drive Bianca and the baby home, Leila can accompany them. But let lightning strike me dead if I climb into a car of a filthy *mundukuru* man whose anus farts violence."

After about an hour Bianca, and Leila carrying the baby, with Abbas leading the way, prepared to go home. "You can go ahead. I want Riti's wounds to be dressed," said Riti's mother. Abbas looked remorseful and ashamed.

"As I was saying," Riti's mother continued, "Juba is no longer a safe place for you to live in, my son. You were not born a man by accident. You must act, and act swiftly before it is too late. You must remember that you are your father's legacy."

Mother and son walked home silently, as if subdued, but defiant against the odds.

After the baby was named and Bianca was back on her feet to do house chores and to fetch water, Riti asked for a conference with her.

Bianca was nursing little Abbas when Riti started.

"Sister, what has happened is behind us. Such is fate which comes in different shades of design. I don't feel safe anymore in Juba. After coming out of detention no one will want to associate with me. I'm only left with one option. I'm now ready to fly to Khartoum."

74

His was a statement. He was not begging.

The baby cried as if protesting his uncle's plan to go away. Bianca rocked him and reached for her cleavage to pull out a healthy breast full of milk. She directed the nipple into the baby's twitching lips. He kept quiet as he sucked his mother's milk.

"Riti," said Bianca as she examined her overgrown nails, "You would have been a dead man, but I tried my level best to get you out. I'm sorry that I'm carrying shame in my arms, but it is shame and abuse that saved your life, Riti. I cannot go into details, because it hurts. I'll remain with the shame for life. Just tell me what day you want to go to Khartoum, I'll ask somebody to fly you out. But come that day, I'll escort you to the airport so that nothing fishy happens again." She stopped there and sobbed. With her left hand she waved at Riti to go out.

Riti walked to his room with his head bowed. His chest swelled with anger. He remembered what the rebel leader once said on radio: "Anger is the best weapon for a freedom fighter."

He stood in the middle of the room that would soon cease to be his. I'm going, he said to himself as if addressing the room. I'm going to Khartoum. I'm not running away. I'm taking the liberation struggle to Khartoum. I'm going to fight for the liberation of my people. I'm going to hunt for that traitor called Sara. She used sex as a weapon of war to lure me into the crocodile's jaws. I defied untimely death. I defy oppression of any nature. I'll fight for freedom. *Aluta continua*!

www.ingramcontent.com/pod-product-compliance
Lightning Source LLC
Chambersburg PA
CBHW030655110726
47901CB00002B/720